The Arrangement

MD
Jean-Pierre

This is a work of fiction. The characters, incidents, places, and dialogues are products of the author's imagination and are not to be construed as real. Any resemblance to any actual events or persons is entirely coincidental.

Cover design by Flomas Studio

This book is dedicated to my late father, Frederic Jean-Pierre and Ralph Jean-Pierre. They are no longer with us but will live forever in our hearts.

Table of Contents

CHAPTER 1

A Ride Back Home

This September morning was nothing like the song. Arius sat alone on the bus in Atlanta, Georgia lost in his thoughts. It has been nearly two years since he returned back home to New York City. A thirty-four-year-old attractive divorcee with a warm brown complexion and dreamy wide-set brown eyes. For once a conservative guy, he sure didn't look like one. His hair had outgrown his stylish cut and his thick beard needed more than a trim. This was not the norm for Arius who was always well-groomed.

Right now, grooming was the last thing on Arius's mind. He was too consumed with thoughts of why he left town. His happiness came to an abrupt end when the woman who he believed was his soulmate did the unthinkable. He'd to relive that day in his head every day. Nothing could erase the vision of what he saw when he came home early from a business trip. Seeing his wife in bed with his cousin was the ultimate betrayal. She showed no remorse leaving Arius on the same day. It did not help when they got married immediately after the divorce. The final dagger in his heart was them welcoming their son into the world last year.

Arius and his ex-wife tried for three years to get pregnant with no success. It only confirmed to him that the problem was him. Not only could he not satisfy his wife, but he was infertile. The thought of him being infertile made him dolorous. His whole life all he ever wanted to be was a father with a house full of kids. He remembered his parents' joyous house with his younger brother and sister. These days, his relationship with his brother and sister was distant. He loved them but they remained friends with his ex.

He felt like his whole family turned against him, except his Aunt Brianna and Uncle Darius. His aunt stood by his side and moved in with him after the divorce to keep an eye on him. He could not have bounced back without her. When Arius' favorite uncle Darius in Georgia got diagnosed with cancer, he took the opportunity to leave town to be there for him. He watched his uncle fight a heroic battle, but three months ago his battle came to an end. Arius put all his uncle's affairs in order and now it was time for him to face his demons back home.

The passengers started loading the bus, but not fast enough for Arius. He wanted the ride to begin, so he could lose himself in the scenery. He noticed a fashionable young lady in her twenties holding her baby in her arms while she argued with an older black businessman. The young lady resembled a model coming off a runway. She wore a light blue denim pair of nicely fitted jeans, a white lace tank top, a red waist-high blazer, and red pumps. She was definitely an eye turner with a light-golden brown complexion and auburn hair blowing with the wind. Arius could sense things were going to get ugly. The man kept putting a paper in front of the young lady's face and hit the baby by accident. Her baby started to cry. She put her baby back in the stroller and got in the man's face.

"Don't you ever put your hand on my baby again!" the young lady yelled.

"I apologize, but I need you to sign these papers. My client does not want you coming back in the near future to sue him," the man insisted.

"Your client should have thought about that before he messed up my life. Do you think a little compensation is going to fix my life? I have to care for my son for the next eighteen years." She was furious with the man who was obviously doing his job.

He pulled out a pen from his pocket and grabbed her hand. "Just sign these documents so I could be on my way."

She tried to wrestle free, but his grip was tight. "Let me go before I knock you out," she demanded.

"You heard the young lady." Arius stood firmly behind her.

She turned to stare at the tall, dark, and very handsome stranger. He was an attractive guy with a strong jawline and beautiful teeth to match. She did not picture him much of a fighter with his slacks and a buttoned-down shirt. The least he could have done was take off his reading glasses before playing a hero, she thought. Their eyes met studying each other. Her dazzling upturned-shape marble brown eyes looked right through him. For a moment, he was completely mesmerized.

"Why don't you mind your own business!" the older man insinuated.

"She is my business. Now, do I have to repeat myself?" Arius tightened his face. The man let go of her hand.

"I could fight my own battles, professor," she said to the stranger.

"I am sure you can, but the bus to New York City is about to leave." Arius wondered if he made the right decision to get involved.

"All she has to do is sign these papers so I can be on my way," the older man repeated.

"What she is going to do is get on the bus, so the bus can leave. You can give her the papers, and she will read them during her leisure." Arius barely got into altercations with anyone, but he felt the need to defend this stranger.

"The return address is on top of the page. Mail it back asap." He threw the papers at her and walked away. She took the papers and stuffed it in the diaper bag.

"Are you going on the bus heading to New York?" Arius asked her.

"Yes, I am. Thank you for helping me." The young lady was too embarrassed to look at him in the eyes.

"No need to thank me. The bus driver said that he is leaving in five minutes. Do you need any help getting on the bus?" There was a kind nature about him when he spoke to her.

"Your help would be appreciated. I have only one bag and a car seat to put underneath the bus."

"I can do it for you. Take your baby out the stroller, so I can put the stroller underneath too."

"Thank you," she whispered softly, as she unbuckles the seatbelt off her baby. "Time to get on the bus, Darius."

"Is your son's name Darius?" Arius gushed over the sweet baby.

She nodded, "Why?"

"I knew someone dear to me with that name. My name is Arius. What is yours?"

"Layla." She was as pretty as her name with her round face and those seductive eyes that left him hypnotized. Her nose was small but straight and her red fire lipstick made her perky lips more alluring than her eyes.

"Beautiful name. Nice to meet you." They shook hands. "You better get on the bus," he suggested.

Layla got on the bus with her baby while Arius put her stuff underneath the bus. When he got back on the bus, she was sitting in his seat. He scratched his head.

"I am sorry. Is this your seat?" Her eyes were teary.

"It was. I am sure there are more seats." He looked around for another seat.

She put her diaper bag on the floor in front of her and said, "You could sit here if you don't mind."

Arius took a seat next to her. "Thank you."

Before she could say a word, tears rolled down her cheeks. She stared out the window so Arius would not see her cry.

"You look like you could use this." Arius handed her a tissue, but the baby grabbed it first. "This is not for you, Darius." He took the tissue back and placed it in Layla's hand.

"Thank you. This has been an overwhelming day." She continued to cry. He watched her cry for a few minutes while she held her baby.

"I can hold him for you while you let it all out."

The only person her baby knew was her. She looked into his trusting eyes and handed him the baby.

"Hi, Darius. You are a good baby for mommy."

Layla stared at her baby and started bawling again. Arius let her cry, as he played with Darius.

Ten minutes later, Layla dried her eyes and blew her nose. She took a wipe out of her bag to clean her hands and face. "I will take him back now."

He looked at her swollen red eyes and felt sorry for her. "I could hold him for as long as you need."

"I think I have cried it all out. Thank you." She opened her arms and Darius jumped back into them. "You already miss your mommy?" She kissed his chubby cheeks.

"He is a sweet baby. How old is he?"

"Darius is six months old. He is very alert for his age," Layla bragged about her baby.

"I can see that. He was listening to me talk to him as if he understood me."

She smiled at her baby.

"The first smile from mommy," Arius announced.

"There isn't much to smile about. Only Darius can get a smile out of me."

"You are too young not to have anything to smile about. How old are you? About twenty-five or twenty-seven?" Arius inquired.

"Are you trying to pick me up?" she speculated.

He was stunned by her question, "No! You just look young," he explained quickly.

"I was just kidding. Thanks for the compliment. I turned twenty-nine years old last week."

"Happy belated birthday, Layla."

"There is nothing happy about it," she agonized.

"Maybe when you get to New York, you will be happy."

"If that was true, then I wouldn't be on this bus in the first place going back to New York."

He understood what she meant.

She turned around and stared out the window. They sat quietly for what seemed like hours, but it was only a half an hour. Arius could not keep his eyes off of Layla. He wondered if her story was as dismal as his for leaving New York. Little Darius kept pulling on his sleeves. He wanted to play some more with Arius.

"Darius, stop pulling on the professor's sleeve," Layla finally said.

"That is the second time you called me the professor. Do I look that nerdy to you?"

"You definitely don't look nerdy. I wanted to see if you were paying attention the way you keep staring at me."

"I am sorry for staring. I was wondering why you left New York," Arius studied her fragile face.

"Brooklyn used to be my home until I let down someone very special to me who tried to help me."

"How did you let them down?"

Layla wondered if she should answer his question or stop talking to him. She decided to continue conversating. "They wanted to help me change my wild ways and I agreed to something I was against. At the last minute, I broke my promise to them."

"That is not worth you leaving town for." Arius saw the guilt in her eyes.

Layla thought about why she was telling a complete stranger her business. She sat quietly for a few minutes.

"I am sorry that is none of my business," he attempted to apologize.

"I thought I was your business." They both laughed.

It has been a while since Layla had an adult conversation, especially with a handsome polite guy. "Almost two years ago, I answered this ad to become a surrogate for a couple in Georgia. It was going to help me pay a twenty-five thousand dollars debt I owed for breaking my promise," she paused. "It is a complicated story."

"Let's back it up a little bit. Who do you owe twenty-five thousand dollars to? Do you have a gambling problem?"

Layla laughed. "No, I don't. I owe someone who wanted to do what was best for me. The saddest part about it, my father believes that I ran off with a guy."

"Why would your father believe that you ran off with a guy?"

"I had a wild past, and my father is a strict Catholic. That is the only reason he would ever believe."

"Okay, back to the surrogate story. So, you became a surrogate and then decided to have your own baby?" Arlus tilt his head back in perplexity.

"Darius is the baby that I carried."

"Are you telling me that you decided to keep the couple's baby? Is that why you were arguing with that man?" Arius was beyond intrigued by Layla's story.

"I told you that it was a long-complicated story."

"We have about fifteen hours before we get to New York. It will make the time go by faster with long complicated stories," Arius indicated.

"If I share my story, will you share yours?" Layla was too familiar when a man had something to hide.

"What makes you think I have a story to share?" was he that obvious, he thought?

"Why would you be on a bus going back to New York? You look like a guy who could afford a plane ticket, but you choose to take the long way home," she read him well.

"I will share my story, but your story better be good."

"Trust me, it is fascinating." Layla turned her focus on her baby who started fussing. "He is hungry. I need to feed him." Layla covered herself with a blanket, as she started breastfeeding.

Arius turned his head around.

Layla observed a bashful Arius. "You probably have seen hundreds of breasts before," she taunted him.

"What am I, a regular at a strip club?"

Layla let out the biggest laugh ever. Arius was not amused.

"You said it, not me. I am thankful I am able to breastfeed," she commented.

"I heard it's very beneficial to the baby." Arius had no idea why they were having a conversation about breastfeeding.

"It sure is. No one tells you that your nipples increase too." Layla continued to inform an uncomfortable Arius. "One day after I breastfed Darius, my nipples were as long as half my pinky. I thought my nipples were deformed. Thank goodness my doctor told me it was normal."

Arius was clueless to why she was sharing such detailed information with him. "How do you have such a private conversation with a stranger? I could be a pervert," he expressed his concern to a giggling Layla.

"You are a good-looking pervert," she was quite taken by his shyness.

"There are some conversations you do not have with a complete stranger. Especially sexual ones." He shook his head.

"How is my nipple story, a sexual story?"

"Don't you think a story like that could turn a man on?"

"Are you turned on?"

Arius was befuddled.

"Trust me, I could turn on a man without a breastfeeding story."

He could see why. Not only was she beautiful with her enticing eyes, but her body was beyond sexy.

"If you say so." He felt no need to contribute to the conversation any longer.

"People often call me Betty Boob. Beautiful, sexy, and sweet."

"How do we start talking about breastfeeding and end up with Betty Boob?"

"I was just sharing an interesting story with you. Seriously, I hope you don't mind me breastfeeding."

"Your baby has got to eat," Arius said while Darius played peek-a-boo with him. He lost all focus with Layla's exposed breast in his face.

"I don't usually cover him. He thinks you are playing with him."

"I will turn around to give you some privacy."

"Don't do that!" she screamed. "He will follow you with my breast in his mouth."

Arius wondered if he would survive this bus ride. After Darius ate, she burped him and changed him on her lap. A few minutes later he fell asleep.

"I can hold him while you finish your complicated story."

She gave him Darius. "What was I up to?" she asked him.

"Darius is not the couple's baby."

Layla adjusted her breast in her bra before she continued. Arius was amazed by how comfortable she was around him.

"You are an attentive listener." Layla was impressed. Usually, most men were attentive to her sexy body. "Not only did they want me to be a surrogate to carry their child, but they also wanted my eggs because the wife had damaged ovaries. I agreed to it for an additional fee. It took a couple of tries before the procedure was successful. The couple were so elated. A week later, the doctor informed me that there was a mix-up at the lab. The sperm they used was not of the husband, but of someone who no longer wanted their semen to be kept frozen."

"How could such a mistake happen?" Arius was astonished.

"Apparently, the names got mixed up. The couple refused to take responsibility for the baby. The next thing they were telling me was to abort the baby and to do the procedure again. I refused to," her face saddened.

"What made you decide to keep a stranger's baby?"

"Trust me, I never saw myself as being a mother. I was a party girl. Having a baby was not in the cards for me."

"Why didn't you abort him?"

"Like I told you earlier, my father is a strict Catholic. He raised me with certain beliefs and values that I never cared about until I had a baby inside of me." Layla touched Darius' cheek.

"I cannot imagine a woman like you so happy being pregnant."

"The pregnancy was a nightmare. I was alone and unrecognizable. My beauty has always been what got me everything in life. Could you imagine how I felt losing it? I turned three shades darker. My lips were bigger than my head and feet were bigger than Shaq's." Layla delineated in detail.

"That's a graphic description."

"Graphic but true. I cried myself to sleep every night. The thought of having a baby drained me. Bringing a baby into this world was a big deal. I was indecisive about my future and his. To top it off, I scheduled a c-section to preserve my most valuable asset and I was crowning by the time I got to the hospital."

"I am sure your valuable asset is still in good condition," Arius stated to be supportive.

"How can it be in good condition after the stretching it went through. Look at this head," she said pointing at Darius' head. "That came out of me. He was almost nine pounds. What chance does my valuable asset have? I will never have another baby again."

Arius felt it was safe to change the subject. "You were going to give the baby up for adoption? What changed your mind?"

"That was the plan at first. I hoped the couple would change their mind. As the months went by and Darius started kicking, I became attached to him. I started to love someone besides myself. After he was born, his little hand clung onto my pinky finger tightly. He was so adorable. He resembles my father a little bit. It was hard for me to let him go. I immediately felt loved by him. I am not a good person, but he makes me a better person."

"Aren't you afraid the donor will want to share custody?"

"The clinic told me the donor would claim the baby if I decided to put him up for adoption."

"You never heard from the donor after you decided to keep Darius?"

"I got some papers from his lawyer giving up his rights."

"Do you know who he is or his name?"

"He wanted to stay anonymous."

"Who was the guy that was arguing with you at the bus stop?"

"He works for the fertility clinic. They want me to sign additional papers keeping them from being liable for my baby. The clinic said they covered all my medical costs during the pregnancy, but I believe it was the donor. I even received a cashier's check compensating me with half the money I was supposed to get as a surrogate."

"That is one outrageous story. Do you plan to sue the clinic?"

"I have enough money to take care of Darius for a few more months. I don't want to waste all my money on court costs. I just want to raise my baby in peace with my family, if they will give me a chance."

"Your family will welcome you and Darius with open arms."

"My father will never believe how Darius was conceived. He will believe that I disrespect his name and worry about what people will say about him."

"He loves you and he will forgive you in time."

"You do not know my father and my stepmother; they will worry about my bad influence on their teenage daughters. Not only am I the wild child, now I am also the unwed child with a baby."

"Did you try to call your father?"

"I tried to call him several times and he hung up on me. I wanted so much to tell him about his grandson. I have been alone for almost two years.

Do you know how it feels when a loved one turns their back on you?" she saw the answer in his eyes.

Arius was unsure if he wanted to share his story with her. It would mean he would have to relive it all over again.

CHAPTER 2

A Juicy Story

Layla had no doubt Arius knew what it felt like for a family member to turn their back on you. He wondered if he should tell her his story. He has always been a private man who kept his pains and sufferings to himself. Why should he share his painful story with her?

"You do know what it feels like. What is your story, Arius?" Layla requested.

"My story is not as interesting as yours, but it would be rude of me not to contribute after you shared your story with me." He smiled at her and handed the baby to her. He took a deep breath before beginning.

"I have a feeling it is going to be a juicy story." Layla waited anxiously.

Arius laughed nervously. "Nothing about my life is juicy, but your story was good. I am a man of my word and I will tell you my story." He was a very attractive man of his word. His eyes were so sincere, and his smile was so sweet. Layla was smitten.

"I have been going back and forth to Georgia for almost a year when my uncle revealed to me, he had been battling lung cancer. He was only sixty-five years old with so much life left in him." Arius paused from grief. "Anyway, when he got worse, I stayed with him for about a year until he passed away three months ago."

"My deepest condolences to you and your family. Why were you still in Georgia after he passed away?"

"Thank you. My uncle had a few requests of me that I tried to accomplish, but I wasn't successful."

"I am sorry to hear. You must feel like you let him down."

"I would have done anything for him. He was a loner who stayed to himself. He never got married or had any kids. He was my favorite uncle. He taught me everything I know. His passion in life was entertaining people. He was a movie producer/writer, and he won several awards for his original works. Since I was a child, he used to tell me the funniest stories. In the end, I told him all the same stories to comfort him," Arius' eyes filled with tears.

"It must have shown him that you were listening."

He remembered his uncle telling him that. "That's exactly what he told me," he hesitated for a moment as he saw his uncle's face in front of him. That is when he decided to continue. "The real reason why I left New York was because my life as I knew it no longer existed. I found my wife in bed with my cousin. He was my best friend. Our friendship meant nothing to him. My ex left me the same day to be with him."

"I told you this was going to be juicy." Layla smacked him on his arm. "Did you beat him up badly and had to leave town? Have you been laying low from the cops?" Her vivid imagination went wild.

"It's not that juicy."

"At least tell me that you kicked your cousin's butt."

"I am the opposite of you. I think first and act later."

She didn't believe that for a moment. "Did you take off your glasses like Clark Kent and turned into a superhero to beat the crap out of him?"

He could see the enthusiastic beam in her eyes. "When you put it that way, I guess I did. He had it coming to him." Arius reminisced about the satisfaction he got out of it.

"What happened after that?"

At this point, he had her full attention. "I dragged our divorce. I wasn't going to make it easy for them to be together. After the divorce, they got married immediately and now they have a child together."

"Did you drag your divorce to get back at her or to give her a chance to come back to you?"

He wasn't too sure of the answer himself. "She was my first love. I thought I was going to spend the rest of my life with her. Maybe if she was remorseful and left him to come back to me. I probably would have taken her back. Honestly, it would have been hard to trust her again. That's when I knew it was over for good." That is also when Arius promised to himself never to give his heart away to another woman to prevent it from being broken again.

"If you knew it was over, then why did you leave New York?"

That was a question Arius has been running from. "My family accepted their relationship. They were welcomed with open arms. They paraded around at family functions like they were the "it" couple. All my family asked me was, 'am I ok'? Like I was a fragile bird."

"That is so disrespectful! I would have cursed everyone out."

Arius could see trouble always followed Layla. "My sister and brother are still good friends with her. My sister is even the godmother to her son."

"How dare your sister take her friend's side over yours?"

Arius shook his head, "I would like to know the answer to that question too."

"Why didn't you have kids with your wife?"

He was not expecting that question to come out of her mouth. He was quiet for a moment.

"Is that a personal question you would rather not answer?"

"Why would it be? We tried as soon as we got married with no success. After the third year, we just put it on hold."

"That's why she cheated on you?"

"I have no idea. She never gave me a reason." Arius was tired of sharing his story.

Layla could see she touched a nerve. "It's hard for me to understand why any woman would cheat on you," she clocked him hard. "You are indeed fine and appealing. Is your package still functional?"

Arius puts his head down in abashment. "Why would I answer such a personal question?" he snapped at her.

"Does that mean no?"

"It means that it is none of your business. I am going to sit somewhere else." Arius became agitated and went to sit in the back of the bus. He didn't expect to react to Layla's comment the way that he did. He always had his emotions under control, but her question hit too close to home. She wasn't the one he was mad at. He was more upset with himself.

The bus ride became boring after Arius changed his seat. Layla felt bad for hurting his feelings. She tried to see where he was sitting to apologize to him, but she was unsuccessful. Maybe he would come back if she gave him some space.

Fifteen minutes later, Arius came back. He sat quietly without saying a word.

"Hi, did you miss us?" A remorseful Layla supplicated.

He ignored her.

"I am sorry for saying anything inappropriate. I got carried away with your story and my loose tongue tends to get me in trouble. It is obvious your package is in working order," Layla tried to make peace.

"How do you know?" He could not believe she would start with the same topic again.

"God would not give such a handsome man a nonfunctional package," she answered.

"You are unbelievable! If you keep talking, I am going to change my seat again."

She grabbed a hold of his arm. "Don't leave us. Do you want a pervert to sit next to us?"

He was captivated by her big brown marble eyes. "I thought you love talking to perverts," he said sarcastically.

"I said you look like a good-looking pervert even with your grizzly beard. You are the exception."

Arius rolled his eyes up. "Now, I am a good-looking pervert. Your foot is getting deeper and deeper into your mouth."

She gave him a warm smile. "If you didn't miss me, why did you come back?"

"It smelled like celery and green onion gave birth back there."

"I smelled celery when I first got on the bus too. I just could not get the second scent."

Arius finally smiled.

"I am sorry for bringing up such a touchy subject. Arius, it is not a big deal if you cannot have children. That would mean good sex with no worries of getting anyone pregnant. Imagine having sex three to four times a day with no fear of pregnancy."

Arius has never thought about being infertile in that way. "Do you ever think about what you are going to say before you say it?"

"I have never got any complaints about the things that came out of my mouth," she winked.

"You should filter what you say. Your wording is very explicit."

"It depends on how the person takes what I am saying. I was only being supportive."

"Then I should take it as a compliment?" he asked.

"I am sure you will not have a problem finding another woman. Look at you," she examined him. "You would be a great catch for any woman. Just let them know your situation from the start. You can always adopt."

"I never thought of it that way, Iyanla."

Layla started laughing.

"What is so funny?"

"I always give people two pieces of advice. I tell women to use the assets their mama gave them and men to pull out their credit cards."

Nothing surprised Arius about the things Layla said.

"Don't listen to me. I am the worst person to take love advice from," Layla added.

"I figured that,"

"So, you ran away because your family still accepts your ex and pushed you out like yesterday's trash."

"That's putting it harshly. I pushed myself out. Seeing them together made me sick."

"All you had to do was hire a sexy escort to go to a family function to show your ex that you moved on."

"I thought you don't give love advice."

"I have never been married, but my side is always for my family. There is no question about it."

"I wish you were a part of my family."

"People become family in the weirdest ways. We can be a bus ride family."

Arius chuckled. "I never heard of bus ride families, but why not."

Layla put her hand out, "As of today, we are family. I will be your little sister."

"Absolutely not," Arius quickly answered. He could never think of her as a sister for many reasons.

"Am I too pretty to be your sister?" she batted her eyes.

Too pretty and sexy, he thought. "Are you that conceited?" he asked a question that he obviously knew the answer to.

"Ok, your cousin?" she suggested.

"How about my backyard cousin?" He shook her soft hand. She stroked his hand in a very intimate way. A few seconds was all he could take before letting go of her hand.

Layla smiled at his timidity. "I hope backyard cousins are not ugly," Layla joked.

Arius smiled.

"Now, I need to get my beauty sleep before Darius wakes up."

"You look like you had enough beauty sleep for a lifetime." He surprised himself with his flirtatious comment.

"Keep it up. Someone will snatch you up soon." Layla observed his fine face. "I am still trying to figure out why your wife cheated on you. You are quite fetching."

"And you are very unique."

"No one has ever called me unique. I hope you mean it in a good way," she yawned. "I better get some sleep while he sleeps."

"I can hold Darius while you sleep. I am not tired yet." His sincere face gave her reason to trust him.

She handed him the baby. "I will sleep for a few minutes," she dozed off right after she finished her sentence.

He watched her sleep for an hour. She had such an innocent face while she slept. Layla rested her head on his shoulder when she tossed, and her hand landed on his leg. As Arius started dozing off, he held the baby tight in his arms to protect him. To anyone observing them, they looked like a lovely family.

Two hours later, the bus made its first rest stop. Arius tried to wake up Layla who was sleeping peacefully with her head on his shoulder and still had her hand on his leg.

"Layla, wake up."

She had no desire to wake up. "Huh," she whispered as she slowly opened her eyes.

"This is the first rest stop. We need to go to the bathroom and get something to eat. Especially you, since you have to feed the baby."

Layla got up and took the baby to the bathroom. She changed the baby and noticed her reflection in the mirror. She had dark circles around her red swollen eyes. How could she be a beautician and allow herself to look like a mess? She decided to multitask by holding Darius and applying some makeup and fixing her hair. A few minutes later, she was all polished up.

When Layla got back on the bus, Arius was waiting for her with some food. He observed her refreshed face as he gave her a burger and fries.

"Thank you. I am famished." She couldn't wait to sink her teeth into the burger.

"You look invigorated," he stared at her radiant face.

"Why didn't you tell me how bad I looked?" her cat eyes urged.

"Because you are too beautiful to look bad."

"Good answer. You are lucky I am your backyard cousin, or else I would snatch you up myself."

Arius was quite entertained by Layla.

An old lady going to her seat couldn't help but stare at the couple. "What a beautiful family," the elderly lady said.

"Thank you," Layla replied instantly.

She continued to admire the two of them. "What a good daddy your husband is. I watched him holding the baby tight while you slept."

"He is the best. He helps me to put the baby to sleep, so we could have our quality time," Layla lied. "Right, honey?"

"Right, sweetheart." Now she was a liar, Arius thought.

"You can't blame him for wanting to have quality time with his beautiful wife."

"Quality time is how we got our baby." They all laughed.

"Enjoy your trip." The elderly lady went back to her seat.

"You are one piece of work, Layla. Your mouth should be appraised," Arius recommended.

"Honey, you have no idea how valuable my mouth is." It was so easy for her to get a smile out of him. "What do you do, Arius?" Layla wondered if he was a professor.

"I am a graphic designer." He noticed the surprise expression on her face.

"I thought you were a professor," she said with food in her mouth.

"Very boring. I am a graphic designer, and it is much more interesting."

"What do you design?"

"I design video games, some features for movies and book covers too."

"Have you ever designed any romance book covers?"

"I have worked with MD."

"Wait a minute, you designed the book covers for the Summer Love Series?"

"Yes, I did. MD sent me a copy of the books afterwards. I actually enjoy reading romance novels now."

"Her books are amazing. I can't wait for book three to come out."

"You will like it," Arius bragged.

"Oh my God, you read it already?"

He nodded, "Maybe one day I will let you read my copy."

"Maybe? You better." She pushed him.

He enjoyed seeing the enthusiasm in her eyes. "Ok. Don't beat me up," he joked. "What is your occupation besides telling complicated and inappropriate stories?"

Her sparkling eyes smiled at him, "I am a beautician."

"I should have guessed the way you are so well put together."

"Are you flirting with me, Mr. Graphic Designer?"

"Don't let it go to your head. Did you work as a beautician while you were in Georgia?"

"Around my second month of pregnancy, I got a job working at the Golden Years nursing home. I would do the senior's hair, makeup, and sometimes their nails. It made them feel good."

"Did you say Golden Years nursing home?" Arius was astonished.

"Yes. I only went in three times a week. I got a chance to meet some nice people. Why?"

"My uncle was there before he got real sick and went to the hospital."

"What is his name?"

"Darius,"

She was shocked.

"They called him Uncle Darius," they both said at the same time.

"Did you know him?" Arius inquired.

"Who didn't know Uncle Darius? He is an amazing man." Layla remembered Arius spoke about his uncle that passed away. "Was he the uncle that passed away?"

He nodded sadly. She became teary. Arius was surprised by her reaction.

"I shaved him and did his nails while he told me some hilarious stories," she mumbled with tears dripping in her mouth.

"Wait, you are Cindelala." His uncle gave Layla a nickname. "He said the prettiest princess came and polished me up. He never said you were pregnant."

"He was so sweet. One day I told him my crazy story. He was so supportive, and he told me that everything was going to be alright. I was at my early stage of pregnancy when I met him. He always looked forward to seeing me. He said I resembled his first true love who died in a car accident."

"He told you about Lalita?" His uncle only told him and his aunt about Lalita.

"He spoke about her a lot. He never got over losing her and his baby."

"My uncle never told me that she was pregnant."

"She was two months pregnant when she died in a car accident."

"No wonder he never got married or had any children."

"He said his love died with her."

"You definitely made an impact on him if he shared such a sentimental story with you."

"We shared our most confidential story with each other. He never judged me."

"That's what I loved about him. When I told him what happened with my ex, he gave me a hug and told me one day I will find the woman I was meant to be with."

"He had a big loving heart. I remembered when I felt sad about my appearance, he told me how beautiful I was. After I had the baby, I brought Darius to meet him, but they said he went to the hospital."

"He got too sick to stay in the nursing home. From the hospital, he went straight to a hospice home."

"He was so amiable to me. He even told me I would be a good mother and..." Layla started to wail.

Arius put his arms around her and held her tight. She showed more affection for his uncle than most of his family. He took a tissue out and wiped her tears. She was taken by his compassion towards her.

"And what else?"

"He said that the right man would find me one day and make me happy again." Layla continued to cry.

"My uncle wanted the best for everyone except himself. He was a selfless guy."

"That's why I named my baby after him. He was the best father figure I needed at that moment. He was sweet, supportive, and understanding."

Arius was lost for words.

"What are you thinking about?"

"You made quite an impression on my uncle. He mentioned you several times."

"What did he say?" Layla was curious.

"I thought he was telling me one of his outrageous stories when he spoke about you. He sounded like he was talking about a fairytale. He called you Cindelala. Honestly, I didn't think you really existed. I understand now what he was talking about." How could Arius put into words what his uncle told him and what he asked of him.

"What? Tell me, Arius," Layla was anxious for answers. She put her hand on his. He felt an instant sensation go through him.

"He said for me to find you."

"Find me for what reason? Was I the request that you could not accomplish?" Her eyes were so distracting. He could barely focus.

"You paid attention. I am touched." Arius wondered if he should share the information with her. "He said some outrageous things like we can help each other with our problems. I thought my uncle was delusional. He told me that you would go back to New York in September. I went to the bus stop since the ending of August to look for Cindelala."

"You were that determined to find me? How can we help each other?"

"We can help each other based on what we are going through."

She listened to him carefully.

"This whole day has not been a coincidence. My uncle has brought us together for a reason."

"Are you saying our encounter was spiritual?" Layla asked interestingly.

"Do you believe in spiritual encounters?" Arius returned the question.

"I am embarrassed to say yes."

"I was sitting on the bus dreading going back to a life that I ran away from. I saw you arguing, and something told me to go help you," Arius explained.

"Something or someone?"

An eerie air surrounded them.

"I guess someone."

"What is the reason?"

"Let's play around with this. What would be the only reason your father will forgive you?"

"If God asked him to," Layla laughed.

"Can you please be serious for one second?"

"Ok, Mr. Serious. He would maybe forgive me, if I came back home a respectable woman. Which is so not possible with a baby in my arms."

"It is possible," Arius declared.

"I am lost. What is your reason for you to deal with your problem?"

"Like you said earlier, by bringing a special lady to a family function to convince my family that I am not a fragile bird."

"Are you saying we pretend to be a couple?"

"We can go further than that by coming up with an arrangement to fix our problems and then annul it after a certain period of time. Your father will forgive you and my family will see that I have moved on from my broken heart with a hot new wife and a baby." Arius could not believe he called her hot.

"You think I am hot?" The feeling was mutual, Layla secretly thought.

He blushed, as she observed his handsome face.

Why was she even entertaining the idea? Her problems were too big for an arrangement to fix. "That is the craziest thing you have said this whole bus ride."

"You are right. I was just thinking out loud."

Layla couldn't help but to consider Arius's idea. "It is an interesting idea, but my father is a smart man. He is not gullible. He wouldn't be easily convinced, and my problems are more complicated than you know."

Arius has always been a thinker, now he was talking about a crazy idea he did not think through. An idea that was not his alone. "Forget I said anything," Arius decided to keep his crazy idea to himself.

They both sat quietly thinking about what Arius said. Could they help each other get their lives back? Or were they just wishful thinking.

The rest of the ride went quickly as Darius kept them amused. Before they knew it, they were in Times Square exiting the bus.

"It was nice meeting you, Arius. You made the bus ride go by faster."

He was going to miss her craziness. "It was a pleasure meeting you too, Cindelala. Please take care of yourself and my favorite little buddy. And stay away from perverts."

"You are not a pervert. You are very handsome and charming. I hope everything works out for you. If anyone bothers you, remember to give your backyard cousin a call, so I can put them in their place."

"I will remember to do so. We should exchange numbers, just in case you need your superhero to save the day."

They exchanged numbers and for a second they did not want to say goodbye. Layla and Darius gave Arius a group hug. He didn't want it to end. In return, he gave them both a kiss on the cheek.

"I am going to rent a car. I can take you and Darius home if you like."

"Sure. I would hate to go in that filthy subway with Darius."

"I am sure he would enjoy seeing all those people and graffiti."

They both shook their heads.

"Come on, Darius. I am going to take you home in style," Arius stated.

The drive to Brooklyn was a quiet one for Layla. All she could think about is the expression on her father's face when he sees them. He would definitely be furious with her. Her heart started beating faster. Would his heart melt when he sees Darius? Or would he be upset with her?"

Layla froze in her seat when Arius got in front of her house. She thought about all the scenarios that could happen when her father sees her. Did she make a big mistake by going back home? Her nerves were like jumping jacks.

"That's the address you told me?" Arius looked at the brown and yellow two-story house.

"It is, but I can't go in," her eyes filled with tears.

"Everything is going to be alright." He could see the fear in her eyes.

"Everything is not going to be alright. My father hates me. Maybe this was a bad idea for me returning back home."

"Your father will forgive you and welcome you with open arms. Especially after he sees Darius' sweet face." Arius hoped his words would give her the courage to go in.

"You better be right. Let's go." Layla had no choice but to face her father. It was time to make things right.

CHAPTER 3

Let the Games Begin

Arius helped Layla and a sleeping Darius out of the car. She unlocked the house door for them. "Wow, the house still looks the same." Layla remembered the last time she was home. She struggled with her decision to leave before walking out the door.

Arius saw the uncertainty on her face. "Are you okay?"

"I am fine," she consisted.

"Take Darius so I could get your bag and stroller." Arius left.

The small narrow porch was anything but welcoming. Her eyes searched for some sort of connection, instead someone familiar entered the room. A salt and pepper haired older dark-skinned man observed Layla with amazement. He shook his head in disappointment.

"Hi, Pop," a shaken Layla said.

"You are so predictable. I figured when things got bad for you that you would come back home, but I never imagined with a baby. How could you bring more shame to our family?"

"Please let me explain. I would never bring more shame to our family. I missed you, Pop."

"You missed me? After the disgrace you brought on our family. You left my home almost two years ago leaving a letter explaining how you found a job in Georgia. Did that job involve a man?"

"No, it wasn't an actual job. I mean it was." Layla confused herself more than her father.

"Save the excuses for someone who cares. You ran away from your obligations. I became a laughingstock because of your selfish decision. Now you come back with your bastard baby expecting a welcome home parade."

"He is not a bastard. He is your grandson. He has made me a responsible person."

"You a responsible person?" His eyebrows rose. "Nothing will ever change who you are and what you did."

"I have changed for the better. Please give me a chance to prove it." Layla knew it was a waste of her time trying to convince her father that she was not the same wild girl.

"There is only one way you can prove to me that you are responsible," he exclaimed.

"Must we talk about that now. I have been travelling all day with your grandson. We are both tired."

"You want to talk about being tired. I have lost countless nights of sleep because of you. I was embarrassed in front of my dearest friend and my debt has skyrocketed. All because of you. If you are not here to go through with your obligations, then you cannot stay here. Get out!" her father screamed.

Layla feared the worse for her and Darius. She started sobbing. "I am sorry if I brought shame to your name, but I tried to make things right. Please let me explain," she pleaded.

"You ran away from your obligations and you expect me to listen to your pathetic excuses. I want you and your baby out of here now."

"Pop, you would never kick me and your grandson out."

Was her father capable of such a cruel act? This was not the welcome Layla was expecting.

Arius heard yelling outside. Layla did describe her father as being strict, but he was not expecting him to yell at her with a baby in her arms. He wondered how he would react when he got back inside? Will he mind his business, or will he be a superhero to save Layla and Darius once again? He would soon find out.

He startled her father when he entered the house. "Where do you want me to put this, sweetheart?" He decided to help Layla the only way he knew how. To play the game. "Why are you crying, sweetheart?" Arius put his arms around her.

Her father observed Arius wiping Layla's tears. "Who the heck are you?" Her father's harsh tone scared both of them.

Arius looked at Layla before answering. She saw the answer in his eyes.

"Arius," she shook her head.

"I am her husband, Arius Colton. It is a pleasure to meet you." He put out his hand, but her father ignored his gesture.

"It is not a pleasure for me," her father rudely replied.

"Arius, this is my father, Darren Nathaniel."

Arius waited patiently for a handshake.

Mr. Nathaniel snubbed him and addressed Layla. "You are married? What a smack on my face." Layla froze in fear of saying the wrong words.

"It was very spontaneous after we had the baby. I had to make an honest woman out of your daughter." Arius quickly came to Layla's defense.

"An honest woman." Mr. Nathaniel chuckled. "Are you talking about my wild daughter?" Mr. Nathaniel looked at her hand, "Where is your ring?"

"Her ring is too tight for her. Layla has a few more pounds to lose." Layla shoved him. Arius continued, "But she is still the most beautiful woman I have ever met."

"Thank you, honey," was all she could say. Darius woke up and gazed into his grandfather's eyes. "Little Darius is up." Arius said with adoration. He jumped into Arius' arms. "Darius, it is time for you to meet your grandfather."

Layla tried to take Darius who held tight to Arius. "He has your eyes, Pop. Would you like to hold him?"

They waited for her father's response. Mr. Nathaniel studied Darius' face. His grandson had a golden complexion like Layla and a head full of brown hair. There was no denying his big brown eyes were similar to his grandfather's round-shaped eyes. Anyone could see the resemblance. Her father had some reservations to salute his grandson, but Darius quickly jumped into his arms.

"I can't believe you have a baby. Congratulations," he said sarcastically.

Layla embraced her stubborn father. "Thank you, Pop. I wanted so much for Darius to meet his grandfather."

"I will let you and Layla catch up. I have got to go." Arius tried to make a rapid exit.

"Are you just leaving your wife and baby here?" Her father inquired of Arius.

"We just moved back from Georgia and I need to get everything set up for Layla and the baby," Arius said, while his body was running out the door mentally.

"This is just a visit?" Mr. Nathaniel's suspicious glance frightened them.

Arius was out of ammunition, but Layla was warmed up now. "Yes, I am a married lady. I need to be with my husband. I just thought you wanted to spend a couple of weeks with your grandson," a nervous Layla explained.

"A couple of weeks sounds forever, but I will see you and Darius as much as I can." Arius took her in his arms and gave her an awkward kiss on the cheek. Her father looked at them strangely. Layla read his expression and did damage control.

"Honey, there is no need to be shy to kiss me in front of my father." Layla kissed him tenderly on the lips. Arius has been wondering how those perky lips would feel on his. He welcomed her inviting lips and gave her a deep passionate kiss. It has been so long since he kissed a woman other than his ex wife. He felt alive again. Layla's body shivered with exhilaration. She was not expecting the conservative,

Arius to be such a good kisser. They almost got carried away until her father cleared his throat. They pulled away with their heads spinning with delight. Their eyes searched for answers.

"Arius call me later, honey," Layla struggled to say.

"I will sweetheart. Take care of our son." Arius said his goodbyes as the games begin.

Arius arrived home forty-five minutes later. He forgot how crazy the traffic was from Brooklyn to Elmhurst, Long Island. He sat in his car looking at his semi-brick ranch style house. He loved his house, but there were so many bad memories not even redecorating could erase. Was it possible for him to make new memories in it? His uncle told him it was possible before he died. He wondered if it was possible with a total stranger he just met.

Now Arius had to go inside and tell his Aunt Brianna about Layla and Darius. He has never lied to his aunt before. Was it worth him lying in order to help Layla? Arius has never been so unsure of his life. He went into the house to continue the game he started earlier.

His anxious aunt greeted him at the door. "Welcome home, Arius," she embraced him.

"It is good to see you again, Aunt Brianna." He lifted his aunt in the air.

She was elderly with medium brown skin complexion. A petite lady with big chubby cheeks. They had the same wide-set brown eyes, and her joyous smile had a way of warming his heart. It was good seeing her lovely face again.

"There is something different about you. What is it?" his aunt asked. Was it the kiss with Layla that made the difference?

"I am still your same old favorite nephew. I probably look fatigued from the bus ride."

"There is something else. You have a radiance about you." The radiance of a certain Layla. "Anyway, how are you holding up? I know how close you were with your uncle."

"He is in my thoughts every day. I miss him dearly," Tears of grief filled Arius' eyes.

"I hated missing my brother's funeral. My doctor was against me traveling with my heart problem and I can barely stand up too long with my arthritis in my ankles." The swellness of her ankles were obvious to Arius. She sat down on the couch.

"Uncle Darius knew how much you loved him." His eyes could not leave her ankles. "Maybe I should get you a home attendant to help you during the day. I don't want to lose you too."

"Don't be ridiculous, Arius. You make me sound old and fragile. I am seventy years old and I can take care of myself," his aunt insisted.

"You are the only family that matters to me now. Your wellness is my priority."

"Arius, you spent two years taking care of your uncle. It is time to make yourself the priority. You need to fall in love and have a life again."

"I do have a life," Arius paused before continuing. "As a matter of fact, I have some good news to share with you." He twinkled.

Aunt Brianna made the sign of the cross and thanked God. "What is it, Arius?" Could it be the news she has been praying for?

"When I first started going down to Georgia, I met someone at the nursing home."

"You met an older woman there?" The thought baffled his aunt.

"No, Aunt Brianna. How desperate do I Look?"

She studied his handsome face. "How could you have met a suitable woman at the nursing home?"

"She was a beautician who worked there. She did the elders' hair, makeup, and nails."

"So, she is a young lady?"

Arius laughed. "She is indeed young and beautiful." Did he just say beautiful? Was he checking Layla out, he thought? "Uncle Darius spent hours talking about her and we finally met. We hit it off right away. We can spend hours talking." That was the truth.

"Why didn't you ever mention her to me?"

"I was afraid it would not work out."

"Stop being so negative. You deserve to be loved after what happened between you and Sierra. Tell me about your new love."

"Her name is Layla, and she is very unique. She has a way with words and can put a smile on anyone's face."

His aunt presumed there was more. "What are you not saying?"

Arius debated whether or not to tell his aunt the whole truth.

"What is my nephew keeping from me?"

"You have always been a mother to me after my parents passed away and my rock after Sierra's affair."

"I am always on your side. I would never judge you."

"The truth is I met Layla on the bus back home, but I knew about her from Uncle Darius."

"Okay, you lost me. You sounded like you have been smitten by her for a while."

Was he? Arius wondered to himself. "Uncle Darius talked about Layla when I went to visit him. The more he spoke about her, the more I was intrigued to find out who she was. Uncle Darius was a fascinating storyteller. He made her sound more like a fairytale character than a realistic person. Come to find out that she is very real. We finally got a chance to see each other today."

"Are you talking about fate or your uncle?"

"Whatever it was, who would have thought we would end up sitting next to each other on the bus. It wasn't until we got to talking about our jobs that we found out our connection. I was blown away." Arius' face lit up.

"That's obvious. Is she that pretty?"

"Not in that way. Her personality is so over the edge and her mouth gets her into a lot of trouble."

"Yet, you are attracted to her. What makes her so special?"

"I am not attracted to her. Stop making something out of nothing. She needs my help because of her wicked father."

"In what way?" Aunt Brianna's curiosity grew.

"I just dropped Layla at her father's house. I told her strict father that we were married because I did not want him to be perturbed with her."

"Why would you lie about that? Why would he be upset with her?"

"She has a wild past and ran away from home two years ago. The last thing her father was expecting was for her to return home with a baby."

"Whose baby is it?"

"It is a long-complicated story."

"I am sure you will tell me one day," she took a deep breath. "How old is he?"

"He is six months old. The sweetest baby I have ever met. He likes me."

Arius' sincerity touched his aunt. "You have bonded with him already. Your eyes sparked when you spoke about him. I know you always wanted kids, but can you raise another man's child?"

"He has no father, and it is not like I could have my own child," Arius stated.

"What are your intentions with this Layla?"

"We intend on helping each other."

"This is the first time since your divorce, I heard you used we in a sentence. How exactly do you two intend on assisting each other?"

"It's too much to get into now. I am exhausted from my trip. I need to know, if you are going to go along with our game?"

His aunt was a church lady who never lied, but she loved her nephew. "I will support you under one condition."

Arius could imagine what that would be.

"Your uncle always had an eye for romance, except for his own. There might be a reason why he wanted you to help her. Maybe helping her, would be helping yourself to heal your broken heart."

He shook his head at his hopeless romantic aunt.

"Don't shake your head at me. I will go along with this game, only if you let go of your past with Sierra and open your heart up to love again."

Arius was not surprised by her request. "This has nothing to do with love. I am keeping a promise to Uncle Darius to help Layla. Where my heart is concerned, I am not ready to love again. Now will you be able to lie to our family, Aunt Brianna?"

"I am a Christian lady who will consider this helping my favorite nephew, not lying to our family." Arius hugged her. "Thank you for telling me the truth. I have a feeling there is more to helping Layla than you are ready to admit. Nevertheless, I can't wait to meet Layla and your baby. By the way, what is your baby's name?"

"His name is Darius."

"Darius!" Her head almost fell off her neck. "After your uncle?"

"Layla and Uncle Darius established quite a bond while he was at the nursing home. They made a big impact on each other."

"It sounds like she made an impact on you too." His aunt was pleased by this impact in more ways than one.

Arius got up. "I need to clean up and check in on Layla and Darius before I go to sleep."

"What a loving husband and father you are!" Aunt Brianna shouted after him.

"Don't start Aunt Brianna." Arius felt good to be home.

The warm shower managed to loosen up Arius' stiff muscles, but his cluster mind needed filtering. He footed around his room with a towel wrapped around his waist. All he could think about were Layla and the promise he made his uncle. How was he going to collaborate the two? He stared at his phone wondering what he was going to say to Layla. How was he going to keep up with this game? A game that started when he found out who Layla was. He decided to wing it and call her.

It did not take long for Layla to answer the phone. "Arius, what took you so long to call?" her words trembled.

"Layla, is everything okay?" he heard the tension in her voice.

"Everything is not alright. What just happened earlier?"

"I helped you out of a messy situation. An old-fashioned thank you will do."

"Thank you for starting a game that neither one of us knows how it will end."

"Relax, Layla. The whole purpose of the game is for your father to accept you and Darius back into his life."

"He definitely accepts Darius, but he is suspicious of us. He keeps asking me questions and I pretend that I am too busy with Darius to answer."

"Good job. Keep avoiding him until I can come up with some answers for him." Answers Arius was oblivious about. "How is Darius doing? I already miss him."

"It's weird. He was looking around for you before he fell asleep. He is fond of you," Layla responded.

"I am fond of him too. I am sorry that I got involved with you and your father's business, but I hate to see a lady cry."

They both were silent in their thoughts.

"Arius, how are we going to convince my father that we are married? He is going to kill me when he finds out the truth." She was skeptical they could pull it off.

"Relax, Layla. Let's not worry about the truth. Let's focus on your father building a bond with Darius. The rest will be a piece of cake."

"It is more complicated than you think." Layla had something to share with Arius, but the guilty feeling in the pit of her stomach would not let her.

"Complicated is my middle name. All will be well," Arius reassured her.

"Are you sure about this, Arius?"

He was more doubtful than her, but he maintained his coolness. "Anything is possible with Uncle Darius on our side."

"He is our guardian angel." A mystic air touched Layla.

They both looked up at the ceiling.

"On another note, my stepmother wants me to invite you to dinner tomorrow. I mean tonight. My father probably put her up to it so they could question us. We might get busted," Layla informed him.

"We will do just fine. Just follow my lead. I have to get some sleep. Please stop worrying about your father."

"That's easier said than done. I..." she was conflicted about bringing up their kiss earlier.

"Do you have something on your mind, Layla?" he was thinking about their kiss too.

"No," she lied. "I better let you go get some sleep. See you later at 6 pm."

"Definitely. Try not to think too hard. You need your beauty sleep." He laughed and hung up.

Layla managed to get a few hours of sleep before her big dinner plans with her parents. She sat in her room thinking how disastrous her evening was going to be. Arius was too good of a man to be involved with her situation. Why didn't she just tell her father the truth? Better yet, tell Arius the whole truth. A truth she came back to face. It was so much for Layla to digest. She decided to focus on a whimsical Darius.

All of the sudden, her sisters, Lexi and Chana came into her room. Lexie was her half-sister who was twelve years old and resembled her father. Chana was her stepsister who was fourteen years old and the spitting image of her mother. Even though Layla was not sure if Chana was her father's child, there was something about her that reminded her of him.

"Layla!" Lexi screamed before seeing the baby. "Is that a baby?" The girls tiptoed into the room staring at Darius.

"Hi, Lexi and Chana. No hug for your big sister?" Layla opened her arms. They stood still. Her sisters were still upset with her for leaving.

"You just left us. You didn't say a word. Just a letter saying goodbye. Big sisters don't do that," Lexie expressed her resentment.

"I am sorry for being such a bad big sister. As a matter of fact, I apologize for all the years I was a selfish big sister. I just partied and hung out with my friends. I never made time for my little sisters. It wasn't until I was away from you that I realized how much of a horrible sister I was. Please accept my apology and forgive me."

Her sisters were mad at her, but they were happy to see her. They ran and gave her a bear hug.

"We forgive you, but you have to promise to be a better big sister," Chana declared.

"I promise."

"Layla, can I please hold him?" Lexi asked eagerly. Layla handed her Darius.

"Please hold his back. He is very active and curious."

Chana waited patiently for her turn.

"He is so cute, Layla. He looks a little bit like dad." Lexi played with Darius as he pulled on her braids.

"Just a little bit," Layla smiled. "It is good to see my sisters again."

"We didn't think we would ever see you again. Dad said some mean things about you," Chana stated.

The last thing Layla wanted to do was involve her sisters in her feud with her father. "Of course, he did. He missed me so much."

Her sisters laughed.

"I can't believe you have a baby. I thought you liked to go out and have fun. I heard a baby is not fun," Lexi commented. She handed Darius to Chana.

"You are right about that. It is hard work when you have a baby." Layla pulled on Lexi's braids.

"Stop, my hair is breaking because I put a relaxer on by myself." Lexie rubbed her scalp.

"Why would you do that? I will get you some hair products to help your hair grow back." Layla hated the inconsiderate person she was before she left home. It was all about her selfish needs. She never had any time for her sisters.

"Thanks, Layla. You are so matured now and prettier than ever."

Layla hugged Lexi. "I guess Darius softened me up. He is such a blessing to me."

"Where is his father? Are you married?"

"His father is my husband of course. We are very happy." Layla bit her tongue. She hated lying to her sisters.

"I thought you said that you never wanted to get married. Did you get married because you got pregnant?" Lexie was direct with her question.

"You are too young for that subject. You should be talking about school. I need to take a shower."

"Can we please watch the baby, Layla?" they begged.

"Put him in the stroller and push him around the room." Layla did not want to take any chances.

"I want to push him first," the girls argued. Layla ran to the bathroom before any negative thoughts came to mind.

CHAPTER 4

Revealing the Truth

The race to get ready was a complex one for Layla who was always tardy. She was unsure what to wear. Arius seems like a guy that would be on time, so she picked the first dress she saw. It was a mustard color double-breasted dress with gold buttons and gold pumps. Layla had a habit of dressing high maintenance thanks to the outlet sales. She curled her hair out and wore a gold headpiece. Her stomach was in knots as she ran downstairs a few minutes before six o'clock. Her feet didn't touch the bottom step when the doorbell rang. Just as she predicted, Arius was an early bird.

"I will get the door." Layla dashed with her high heels without breaking her neck. When she opened the door, Arius took a moment to assimilate the stunning vision in front of him.

"Good evening, Arius." She checked him out in his navy-blue two-piece suit. He was definitely a fine man. He came in with a bottle of wine and two bouquets of roses. Layla gave him a friendly hug.

"Good evening, sweetheart." Arius handed her a bouquet of red roses.

Her nose sniffed the roses. "Thank you, they are beautiful."

"This is a bottle of wine for your father and flowers for your stepmother."

Layla took them and put it on the end table. She immediately pulled Arius in the corner.

"My wife is frisky tonight," he joked.

Layla examined the merchandise in front of her. "You are lucky I intend to behave myself tonight. On a serious note, there was no need for you to bring us anything."

"I wanted to." He couldn't take his eyes off of her. "You look absolutely fabulous."

"Arius, are you checking me out." Any other day, she would flirt with him, but this was not the right time. "I am freaking out too much to engage in a flirtatious conversation with you."

"Am I in the right house? Where is the libidinous Layla?" he jeered.

"Stop it, Arius." She elbowed him. "I need to tell you something I did not share with you on the bus. My father might mention it to you."

"I am sure it won't get in our way," he comforted her.

"Please listen to me."

Arius noticed her father coming their way. "Sweetheart, I have missed you." He took her into his arms and kissed her intensely. She had no time to pull away. Instead, her lips reacted to his kiss by parting as his tongue entered her mouth. She tasted the wine he drank to calm his nerves before coming. He teased her tongue with gentle strokes that drove her insane.

Before their tongues could lock, her father interrupted them.

"You lovebirds need a room."

Arius gradually pulled away to straighten himself out. "Good to see you again, Mr. Nathaniel. Thank you for your dinner invitation. I brought you a bottle of wine and these flowers are for your wife."

Her father accepted his gift. "Thank you. Please come in, so I could introduce you to my family."

Arius took Layla's sweaty hand and followed her father.

"Fiona, this is Arius Colton. Layla's husband."

Fiona was an average looking woman in her late forties with long box braids who wore a lot of makeup to cover her discolorations. "Nice to meet you."

Arius shook her hand. He heard two teenage girls giggling.

"And these are my daughters, Lexi and Chana."

"Nice to meet you," they said.

"It is a pleasure to meet you." Arius shook their hands. He saw Darius staring at him. "Is that my little Darius staring at me?" He kicked his feet wanting Arius to pick him up. He jumped into his arms as soon as Arius undo the seatbelt. "I missed you too," he gave him a big kiss.

"Dinner is ready. Girls could you please help me set up the table and Darren could you please pour us some wine?" They left the room. Layla went to Arius.

"Please stop worrying, Layla," Arius stopped a nervous Layla from distressing.

A few minutes later, they sat down to eat a fried chicken dinner with all the trimmings. They ate quietly until Mrs. Nathaniel addressed the elephant in the room.

"Arius, how did you and Layla meet?" she asked.

"Every time I tell the story I get emotional. Layla worked at the nursing home that my uncle was in. He adored Layla like a daughter." He gazed into her eyes. "One day when I was visiting my uncle, a stunning Layla entered the room. I was enchanted by her presence. As soon as she said 'hi', I knew she was the one." Arius waited for Layla to continue the story.

"When Arius shook my hand, there was an instant attraction. As you could see, he is a very handsome man. His smile warmed my heart. I never felt this way with any guy before," Layla smiled at Arius. "Anyway, he always found a way of visiting his uncle when I was working in order to get acquainted with me. It wasn't until the fifth time we saw each other that he got enough courage to ask me out."

Arius was more taken by the story than her parents. Especially her father who was busy dissecting their story in his head harder than Columbo.

"It took me so long to ask her out because I wanted to do something special with Layla. Finally, I took her to the most romantic southern restaurant in Savannah, Georgia. I remembered that pretty red dress she wore. Her hair smelled like a field of fresh lilies. We talked and laughed the whole night. I couldn't see my life without her after that night." Layla put her hand on his electrifying all of Arius' senses. "And the rest is history." Arius kissed her on the cheek.

"That's romantic," Lexi commented.

"What do you know about romance?" Mr. Nathaniel asked. Everyone laughed.

After dinner, Layla went to put Darius to sleep while Layla's father took Arius into the living room to talk.

"Please have a seat, Arius." Mr. Nathaniel sat on his reclining chair and Arius sat on the couch across from him.

"That was a delicious meal your wife cooked. Thank you for inviting me."

"It was my wife's idea. It has given us a chance to get to know you." He adjusted the recycling chair to get comfortable. "That was a sweet story you and my daughter shared with us. Too bad sweet encounters and my daughter does not mix. Maybe crazy and wild."

He was right about that, Arius thought. "Layla has definitely brought excitement into my life," Arius spoke the truth.

"My daughter knows how to use her assets well. You look like a man of honor, so let me reveal the truth about my daughter--"

"Layla told me about her past and it does not matter to me," Arius was not interested in his truth.

"You decide for yourself after you hear what I have to tell you."

Arius had no choice in the matter, so he sat back and listened.

"My daughter graduated in the top ten of her class. She is smarter than she looks. Her mother left me a couple of months before her graduation. We never heard from her again. A year after Layla started college, she partied more than studied. Her grades diminished and she dropped out of school. She got a job as an assistant manager at a McDonald's to pay for beauty school, but my daughter had other resources to help her," he winked at Arius. "She would shop by day and party from Thursday to Sunday night. I tried to get her to change her reckless ways with no results. Finally, I found a solution to end her wild ways."

"What did you do?" Arius was certain that he would not like his answer.

"My daughter spent most of her life getting what she wanted with her pretty look. An old friend came over to see me and saw Layla. He was captivated by her beauty and felt she would be a suitable bride for his son who was getting too old to give him grandkids. They are a well-off family with old money. I had some debts to pay off and I wanted my daughter to have a secured future. It was like killing two birds with one stone. Layla agreed and they gave me twenty-five thousand dollars to pay off my debts. Everything was in order until a week before the wedding, Layla ran off leaving me humiliated and in debt."

"Your solution to clear your debt was to sell your daughter and you ended up humiliated? I am glad she ran away," The veins in Arius' inflated.

"I was trying to save my daughter's reputation," her father became defensive. "You have no right to judge me. I am impressed by your loyalty to my daughter, but she will never change her ways. I have a strong feeling you two are not married. You need to show me proof. If that is the case, then she will marry my friend's son as planned. Claude has waited patiently two years for her. I signed a contract that Layla agreed to. I do not have the money to pay them back and my reputation has been ruined because of Layla."

Arius was dumbfounded by Mr. Nathaniel's words. "You signed a contract selling your daughter for twenty-five thousand dollars and now you want to force her to marry a man she does not love. The only person that is obligated to this contract is you. You spent the money, and now you need to pay it back."

"I have other obligations. I have lost enough because of Layla. Every day my debt is increasing with interest. I will not lose my home. I have a family to think about with two teenage daughters."

"Will you arrange for them to get married too or selling one daughter was enough?"

"How dare you? I will do whatever I need to do for my family and Layla is the answer to my problems. Now you can stop pretending my daughter means anything to you and leave before you get your heart broken."

"Not before I say good night to Layla." Arius went upstairs without his permission. He found Layla rocking Darius to sleep. Layla could imagine what her father said to Arius to put such a frown on his face.

"What's wrong, Arius?" she was concerned.

"Please put the baby down, so we can talk."

She did as he instructed. "Did my father tell you everything?"

"You could say that. Why didn't you tell me the real reason why your father disowned you?"

"I tried too earlier. I was too embarrassed to tell you on the bus."

"I want to hear your side of the story." They sat down on the bed.

"Let me start from the beginning. My mother left my father when I was a senior in high school. My life spiraled after that. It didn't take my father long to remarry someone else. Fiona is a good stepmother and treated me like her own child. My father, on the other hand, took all his anger out on me for my mother leaving him. He constantly compared me to her because I resembled her. He said that I was a wild woman like her.

"So that is exactly what I became. I partied hard and did other things that I am ashamed of. My father felt I was ruining his good name and decided to do something about it. His old school friend came over and he was mesmerized by my beauty. He told my father that I would be the perfect bride for his aging son. My father was skeptical at first because he knew I was a party girl, not wife material. That was until they offered him money. It was his answer to paying off his debts he made going to the Casino. Anyway, we fought about it until I finally agreed."

"Why would you agree to it?"

"Three months after my toxic relationship ended, my father propositioned me about marrying Claude. I was furious at first with my father, but I was so depressed from my breakup that I eventually agreed to marry Claude. I never saw my father so proud of me. It actually brought us closer. A couple of months later, I met Claude for the first time. He was forty-seven years old and not very attractive. He examined me like the best Christmas gift he ever got. He told me all the nasty graphic ways that he intended on pleasing me in bed. I am no angel, but he was a freak. The first and only time he kissed me, he wet my whole face with his sticky saliva. I almost threw up. The worst part about it, Claude wanted us to marry in four short weeks. The closer the wedding day came, the more doubtful I became. That's when I saw the surrogate ad and thought I could solve all my problems."

"By having a baby to get yourself out of the arrangement?"

"By having a baby to help a couple have a child and to pay back my father the money he spent. I felt responsible for my father taking the money after I agreed to the arranged marriage. It was wrong of me to agree in the first place. Before I left, I wrote my father a letter to apologize for my actions and gave him two thousand dollars of my savings."

Arius saw the disgraced expression on Layla's face. "You shouldn't have given him a penny. He had no right to arrange a marriage for you or spend the twenty-five thousand dollars. Did you tell my uncle the reason you left New York?"

"I told him everything in confidence. He hated what my father did. He kept telling me that he wished there was a way he could help me. I thought it was so sweet of him to want to help someone he hardly knew. I told him if I decided to keep the baby, I would return to New York in September."

"Why September? Did you come back to go through with the wedding?"

"When I first got to Georgia, my father called me to curse me out. He informed me that his friend was giving him two years to pay back the money or for me to marry Claude. I thought I would have had the money by then, but the mistake happened. It changed everything."

"Darius is not a mistake."

"You are right about that, but I felt I was being punished for all my past sins."

"Layla, whatever you did in your wild days doesn't have to be punished by you marrying a pervert."

"What else could I do? I lost the opportunity to pay my father back the money. I spoke to my sisters a couple of times and they told me how stressed out my father was because of his debts. All I could picture was them being homeless. I blamed myself for agreeing to the arrangement and then running away. It is all my fault and I have to right this wrong. Even if it means marrying Claude."

"You will not marry, Claude. Let me help you."

"Arius, you have been so helpful, but this is my problem. It will be best for everyone if I go through with the arranged marriage."

"No, you won't. I will not let you marry that obnoxious man."

"We cannot pretend to be married forever. My father will figure it out."

"He already has figured it out. Your father is desperate because of his debt. Let me get you out of this mess."

"You cannot always be my superhero. I have messed up my father's reputation and good name. I can't let him lose his house and have my sisters be homeless. I don't have any other choice."

He saw the fear in her eyes. "You have a choice."

Her eyes searched for the answers.

"Do you trust me?" He saw her answer written all over her face. "I will pick you and Darius up on Friday morning."

"For what?"

"I am taking you out of this house and making you my wife," those were his last words before he left.

CHAPTER 5

Paying A Debt

Layla attempted several times to call Arius, but her calls kept going straight to voicemail. What was Arius thinking when he said that he was going to make her his wife? Does he not expect her to have a million questions? How dare he not discuss it with her? The audacity of him to ignore her calls, Layla fused. She had an earful to tell him if he ever picked up his phone. Layla called for the twentieth time and he finally picked up.

"Hi, Layla," Arius said in a suave voice.

"Hi, Layla," she repeated. "I have been calling you since Monday morning. It is Wednesday afternoon."

"Thank you for the info. I had no idea what day it was," he laughed. He enjoyed taunting her.

"This isn't funny. What did you mean when you said that you were going to make me your wife?"

"Exactly what I said. I am sorry I did not pick up your calls. I have been very busy getting the house ready for you and Darius, the marriage license, and other errands I had to run."

"This isn't a casual conversation. I am still on exactly what I said. I had no idea that was the new way a man proposes to a woman these days. We are not in caveman times. You do not just say what we are going to do, and we do it."

"I can't imagine you during the caveman times, with your high heels and red lipstick," he chuckled.

"Arius!"

"Okay, wildcat. Put your claws back in." He pictured the steam that was coming out of her ears. "I asked you if you trust me and you said yes indirectly. Do you want to marry a complete stranger or your backyard cousin?"

"Don't you throw the backyard cousin in this argument. You are a stranger too. What is the difference?"

"I am not marrying you to use you sexually or to make you a trophy wife."

"What are you saying? This will be a marriage of convenience?"

"This will be an arrangement that will be best for both of us. Your father cannot force you to marry someone if you are already married. You have no idea what contract your father signed with your arranged marriage. You might be forced to oblige by it if you are not married. At least, we could stomach each other, and Darius likes me. Do you really want to bring him around a man he might hate?"

"Darius loves everyone."

"He will not love a man he sees his mother loathe."

He did make a lot of sense, she thought. "What's in it for you? I learned since grade school, there are no free lunches in life."

"I already explained to you that you can help get me off the fragile bandwagon my family has put me on. We can show them that I have moved on with a wife and child. You can also help me with my aunt."

"What about your aunt?"

"She is my uncle's older sister. My aunt Brianna has been staying at my house while I was away. She is too proud to let me get her a home attendant to help her around the house. Since you took such great care of my uncle, maybe you could care for her with your kindness. The same kindness you showed my uncle."

"You want me to be your aunt's home attendant?"

"I am a busy man working on different projects. You could keep her company with your intriguing stories. You could help her in the kitchen and make her pretty. You do have a gift."

Layla considered his offer. "How long do we have to stay married? I mean how long is this arrangement? We will eventually want real love in our lives."

"We will agree on a time that is best for both of us. The big question is, will you marry me and still have a life or marry Claude and lose your life."

Layla did not need much time to decide on an answer. "What time do I need to be ready on Friday?" That confirmed their arrangement. They hung up wondering what the heck did they just agreed to?

Friday morning came like a breeze as Arius got dressed. He wore his best grey Armani suit. Was he actually going to get married again? This was for a different reason, but will he be able to keep his heart out of? His hands trembled as he tried to tie his tie. Aunt Brianna watched from the doorway trying her best not to laugh at her stubborn nephew.

"Do you need any assistance?" his aunt asked.

Arius surrendered and went for help. It only took her a couple of minutes to tie it. "Are you sure this is what you want to do?"

"There is no other way. Do you believe a father would try to sell off his daughter?" Arius told his aunt what happened with Layla's father.

"That is low for any father to do to his daughter. Are you marrying Layla to help her or get back at her father?"

"What kind of question is that Aunt Brianna? Of course, I am helping her. She doesn't want to marry a stranger who will do what he pleases to her. She would be his prisoner."

"What makes you think she won't feel like a prisoner with you. You cannot keep her in a marriage forever. One day she will want her freedom."

"I understand that. I was thinking that maybe two years of marriage would be good for both of us. I will establish a relationship with Darius and hopefully we could part as parents."

"You expect me to believe this marriage is all about Darius. I saw how upset you were when you came home after having dinner with her parents. You care about Layla."

"How could I care about someone I do not know. Look where that got me with Sierra who I thought I knew. I married someone who in my heart was Ms. Perfect. You can't judge a book by its cover." Arius put on his blazer. "Yes, Layla admitted to me about her wild past, but I believe she is trying to better herself because of Darius. Also, Uncle Darius told me that we could help each other. I made a promise to him that I intend to keep."

"I feel like you are not telling me everything," Aunt Brianna sensed there was more to this marriage.

"Trust me, auntie. This is all you need to know for now."

"I will pray for the best outcome for you and Layla. I can't wait to meet them."

"You are going to love them. They are lovable. I mean Darius is lovable."

"I know exactly what you meant," she shook her head.

"Aunt Brianna, I need you to behave yourself."

"I will behave myself only if Layla has no knowledge that I am aware of this arrangement. To me and everyone else, you are a happy couple who are madly in love with each other."

As much as he wanted to disagree with her, she did have a point. Especially with Layla being her home attendant. "You are right, but you still need to behave yourself." Arius checked the time and went on his way.

Layla couldn't believe she was going through with this marriage. Was this a better choice than marrying a complete stranger? She didn't even believe in marriage. Why was Arius so set on helping her? The questions would not stop coming. When did she become such a thinker? She has always been a spontaneous woman who did whatever she pleased. That was until Darius came along. He was her priority. She gushed as she watched him sleep. He was the best part of her and faded all her doubts away.

The time came for Layla to get ready for her big day. Her closet was full of gorgeous dresses she accumulated over the years thanks to admirers and many credit cards. She was thankful that her father did not throw her clothes away after she left.

With so many outfits to choose from, a pearl-colored spaghetti-strapped dress with a diamond V-neck caught her eyes. She wore that dress to her best friend's all white engagement party. It was classy and elegant for the occasion. The silk fitted material embraced her new curves, it was the perfect dress for the arrangement.

Next, she focused on her flawless face. No need to mess with perfection. She simply applied a light powder and red lipstick. Her hair was another story. It has been a month since she did it. Darius consumed all her time. The brown roots were starting to show, but her auburn hair was still stunning. She parted her hair in the middle and wore it out.

Her reflection in the mirror was of a ravishing bride, but inside she questioned being any man's bride. Her troubled mind caused her hands to quiver. It was too late to have any doubts. She put on her jacket to conceal her dress. It was going to be hard enough to face her father, without him exploding about her running off once again. Now this time marrying another man.

By the time Layla got downstairs, her father was waiting for her. There was no avoiding him like she did the whole week. He impatiently watched her put the baby in the car seat before he addressed her.

"Good morning, Layla," her father checked her out.

"Good morning, Pop."

"Why are you wearing a jacket in the house?" He noticed her diamond sheer heels. "Where are you going?" The bags on the floor only confirmed his suspicion.

"Darius and I are leaving." His chest came up as he adjusted his breathing. "Don't look so surprised."

"You would actually run away from your obligations a second time?" He sucked his teeth.

Layla was not at all surprised by his comment. "I am supposed to be obligated to you? What about your obligation as a father?"

He gave her an empty stare.

"Thank you for having none. I will come and get the rest of my things at a later time." Layla spotted the redness in his eyes. She wondered if it was from lack of sleep or frustration.

"You wouldn't dare walk away from your obligations again." She rolled her eyes. "Layla, I beg of you. I am about to lose my house. Do you want me and your sisters to be homeless? Please marry Claude and keep us with a roof over our heads." This was the first time her father has ever pleaded to her.

"Did I ever matter to you, father? I am a mother now with responsibilities. I am not going to marry a pervert. What will happen to Darius?"

"Your stepmother and I could raise him. They do not need to know about Darius. Please, Layla. Claude will provide you with the finest things in life." His desperation was more pathetic than his imploration.

"You would ask me to give up my son for money." The ache in her heart made her shudder. The old Layla would have chosen materialist things in a heartbeat, but she had outgrown her. "Darius is everything to me. I would rather lose you than my child." Layla heard the doorbell. "It must be Arius." She went to open the door.

Arius came in and kissed her on the cheek. "Hi, are you ready for our big day?"

"Not exactly." Layla's eyes popped out of her head by his attire. "Armani suit? I am impressed."

He looked so suave and smelled amazing. "I had to look my best for our arrangement."

"I just threw this old dress on."

"I am sure it is beautiful, even though I cannot see it. Are you ready?"

"I have so many clothes to take, but I have nothing to put them in. I might need to come back another time to get them."

"Get them organized for me. My trunk is clean. I will take as much as I can. Do you mind if I have a few minutes with your father?"

"That's not a good idea. He is upset that I am leaving. He has been begging me to reconsider. He actually told me to leave Darius with him to raise so I could marry Claude."

"He told you that. I just need ten minutes with him." He sensed her unsettled demeanor. "Please don't let your father get to you. I will make everything right." Arius had a final move to make to complete this game.

His confidence ensured her. She embraced her superhero.

"What was that for?"

"Thank you for saving the day. I have a feeling you are a man of your word." She hurried to get all her stuff organized.

Arius and her father got ready to rumble. The coldness in his eyes told Arius that he was not going to let Layla go without a fight. "I guess there is no sense in saying good morning."

"You are making a big mistake interfering in our family business. My daughter has an obligation to fulfil."

"Layla is obligated to her new family now. That's Darius and I."

"You will never turn my wild daughter into a housewife. She will break your heart before the end of the year."

"The way you broke hers."

"She will be back. I am her father. She always returns home."

"This isn't a home. As of today, Layla is my wife and my responsibility." He handed an envelope to her father. "This is for Layla's debt. Don't you ever bother her again. If she decides to give you the time of day, it will be a blessing to you."

Her father peeked in the envelope and was gratified at the amount of the check. "I didn't think you had it in you. Maybe you do have what it takes to keep my daughter's attention for a few months. Trust me, after she finishes seducing you, she will move on to the next victim."

Arius was ready to put him in his place, but Layla came down the stairs. The tension in the room was thick enough to cut with a knife.

"You got everything?" Arius asked. He decided to end the battle for now.

"Yes, but what have I just walked in on?" Layla studied Arius and her father.

"Nothing. We are running late." Arius picked Darius in his car seat. "Let me help you and the baby in the car. Then I will come back for the rest of your things."

Layla turned to her father. "Take care, Pop. You could give me a call whenever you want to see Darius."

Her father embraced her. "We have a bad history, but you will always be my daughter."

"Goodbye, Pop." She picked up her bags and followed Arius.

Layla felt such a hollowness inside of her. A part of her felt like she lost the only parent she had, and another part felt a heavy weight lifted from her shoulders. Arius gave her space to digest whatever was going on in her head. He had a few things going on in his head too. Especially what her father told him about Layla seducing him. Nevertheless, he was ready to go through with their arrangement.

The arrangement got real when Arius parked across the street from the City Hall. Layla bit her nails. Could she really go through with this? She needed more information to seal the deal.

"Are you sure you want to marry me? You are getting over a bad divorce. You do not need me and my baggage stressing you out. Plus, I refuse to let you pay my debt with your hard-earned money. It's my fault and I need to be accountable. I should just marry Claude and all my problems will disappear. Oh, my goodness, this is so overwhelming. My head feels like exploding," her brain was on overdrive.

"Layla, please relax while I get a word in." Arius attempted to calm her. "It has been three years since my divorced. I am prepared for this new chapter of my life. It will be a new beginning for you too." Arius paused as he observed her biting her nails. He removed her fingers from her mouth. "There is no need for you to worry about your father's debt. I will pay your father in installments. I gave him my first payment today. I will pay him each month until your debt is paid off. Your only concern will be caring for Darius and my aunt. This marriage will benefit both of us. Your father has been dealt with. My family will finally stop feeling sorry for me. Our arrangement will bring us both closures," Arius hoped his clarification put Layla's mind at ease.

"I promise to pay you back and I can start with my first paycheck."

"What paycheck?" Arius wondered what she had in mind.

"Being a home attendant is not cheap. We could agree on a payment of two thousand dollar a month. This way I could pay you back."

"That would be me paying myself back. Anyway, it will not be necessary. Your paycheck could go into your savings. You could pay me back by getting me some respect from my family. Trust me, we will help each other mend our broken lives."

"Is that it? Or will you have expectations of me?" After those two kisses, Layla wanted to explore all the expectations.

"If you are talking about your wifely duties, you will have your own room. I would never take advantage of you in that way. I have spent a few years without a woman, I will survive a couple more years." He wondered if he would survive a day after another kiss.

"We are only human and have needs too."

"I could control my needs. We just need to look like a happy couple when we are around our family."

Layla has never been able to control herself around an attractive guy. "You mean kissing and touching." She was determined to squeeze in touching too.

"I don't remember touching you." He did remember feeling the spark of electricity that went through his veins when he held her in his arms.

"We can't look like a real couple without touching." She ached for a touch of a man.

"We can hold hands if that is what you are talking about. If not, are you trying to include something in our arrangement?"

Must she raise a flag? Why must she look like the aggressor? "Not exactly, but how long can a person survive in a marriage of convenience without sex?" Not long for her.

"We can survive a couple of years." Could he after the comment her father made?

"Are you saying this marriage is for two years?" Layla tilted her head back. She knew she wouldn't last a week after their kisses.

"Yes. Do you have any disagreements with anything I have said?"

She had a few, but she held her tongue. If she could spend two years in a city without any family, then she could stay married to a handsome stranger for two years after he helped her. "None."

"Let's get married." They went into City Hall as two complete strangers and came out a married couple. Neither knew what the outcome of this arrangement would be, but they made the sacrifice to assist each other.

CHAPTER 6

The Newlyweds Have Finally Arrived

The bright sunlight blinded aunt Brianna as she stared out the window. It was a beautiful sunny day and the bright-colored leaves on the tree made the day even more spectacular. Definitely a day to get married. Aunt Brianna waited eagerly for the newlyweds to arrive.

The day quickly went dim when she observed the newlywed couple in the window. They seemed more upset than elated. Layla and Arius got into an argument after Arius asked her how it was possible for her to have such an expensive wardrobe. She did not appreciate his accusations and questioned him about his lack of sex life.

They tried to put on a happy mask before entering the house, but no mask could cover the frown on their faces. Neither one noticed the decoration aunt Brianna had put up to welcome them.

"Congratulations! The newlyweds have finally arrived!" Aunt Brianna screamed.

Layla studied the short jolly old woman. She had a pretty, round face with a glorious smile.

"Thank you, Aunt Brianna. You shouldn't have," Arius said absurdly.

"It was my pleasure. I am so thrilled for you two." She hugged the newlyweds.

"Aunt Brianna, this is my lovely wife, Layla," he introduced his distressed wife.

Layla kissed her on the cheek. "It is so nice to meet you," Layla greeted her.

"You are more beautiful than my nephew described."

Layla got that compliment all the time. "Thank you and you are as lovable as I pictured you would be."

His aunt blushed from Layla's kind words. "I like her already, Arius. Where is little Darius?"

Arius put the car seat on the sofa. His aunt pushed him out of the way so she could see Darius' precious face.

"Can I please hold him?" she asked Layla.

"Yes, he loves the ladies." Layla could see Darius was happy to make another friend. "Say hi to your auntie, Darius." He giggled as she cuddled him.

"I will get the rest of your clothes in the car." Arius went to get her things.

"Please have a seat, Layla. How is your day going so far?" Aunt Brianna asked.

Layla took off her jacket before sitting down. "It has been an interesting day. I hope you didn't burden yourself over us."

"I just tidied up and cooked a delicious meal." Aunt Brianna was unable to keep her eyes off a stunning Layla. "Wow, you are such an enchanting bride."

"Thank you. This was the only white dress I had."

"Perfect choice for the occasion. I hope you are hungry."

"I am starving, and the aroma is about ready to give me an... I mean drive me crazy," Layla caught herself before her mouth got her into trouble.

"My food does that to everyone," she grinned. "I hope you like roasted turkey, candied yams, stuffing, baked corn, and rice with peas."

"I am famished and not shy around good food."

"As you can see," Aunt Brianna rubbed on her belly. "Me too. I also made a small cake and sweet potato pudding."

"I think I love you." Layla was close to having an orgasm.

Arius returned with Layla's clothes and caught a glimpse of her without her jacket on. He was spellbound. "Ouch!" he shouted after bumping his foot on the coffee table.

"Arius, you need to focus on where you are going." Aunt Brianna stated.

"I wasn't paying attention."

"What were you paying attention to?" she grinned at him.

"I was happy to see that you already stole my bride's heart." He was delighted they were getting along.

"Arius, your aunt made a cake and sweet potato pudding for us. I am going to lick my fingers." She licked her fingers and Arius swallowed more than his saliva.

"Now, I know how to put a quick smile on my wife's face. I could have used you earlier, auntie."

"Are you sure you two are newlyweds?" his aunt questioned.

Arius put the clothes down and glanced at Layla. "What are you talking about?" Arius asked, giving his aunt a firm look.

"First, you two come in looking like you want to kill each other. Next, I haven't seen one kiss or hug from a newly married couple."

Arius did kiss her on the cheek after the ceremony ended.

Layla stood up giving him an awkward stare. "I wore him out earlier," Layla playfully pushed him.

"She sure did. I am still trying to catch my breath," Arius followed her lead.

"Do you two have something to tell me?"

Arius got closer to Layla. He gave her a quick tap on the lips. She prolonged the kiss as her lips covered his. Her fingers ran through his hair to pull him closer. As their bodies rubbed against each other, they incited a flame of passion. Layla felt a tingling sensation that left her wet in a place that has been dry for far too long. Arius gently pulled away to avoid losing control.

Aunt Brianna applauded them, "I was mistaken."

The kiss confirmed there was more than an arrangement between them. Sparks were definitely present. The kind of sparks that would bring Arius back to life again, Aunt Brianna pondered.

"Now that you are entertained, Aunt Brianna. I am going to give Layla a tour of the house." Arius placed his hand on her waist and guided her around the house.

"This is an open concept house. We were in the living room. Then the dining room and here is the kitchen." It was stunning; white and brown marble countertop and matching island with four stools. The gas stove was the size of two stoves. Layla pictured herself spending lots of time in the kitchen.

"Your kitchen is beautiful."

Not as beautiful as her, he thought. "Thank you. Behind the kitchen is a bathroom, auntie's room, and my office. I do a lot of work in my office, so I don't allow anyone in it."

Layla hoped that did not apply to her.

"Downstairs is a furnished basement. Up those stairs is another bathroom, my room, and the guest room."

She knew which room was hers. "You have a big house for a single guy."

"I fell in love with this house the first time I stepped foot in it. I thought I was going to have a house full of kids."

"You are still young, and Darius can fill your house for the next couple of years."

"It's our house for the next two years."

Layla never felt any house was hers or a place to call home. "Our house?" Their eyes met.

"Layla, you are not in prison. This is your house too. You can do whatever you want in it."

Ideas began to fill her mind.

"You know what I mean. I don't want you to be miserable."

"Thank you." Was it possible this house could be a real home for her and Darius?

"It is time to eat!" Aunt Brianna yelled. They sat down to eat the feast his aunt had made. Arius and Layla offered to clean up after dinner. After they ate dessert, Arius showed Layla to her room.

"If you think the room is too small, then we can switch."

Layla examined the room which was bigger than her bedroom at her father's house. The oak engraved bed frame was breathtaking. Like it was designed especially for her. It was attached to a queen-sized bed with a matching dresser. There was also a rocking chair and a crib for Darius.

"It is perfect. Thank you." She cracked half a smile.

He could tell there was something on her mind. "What is troubling you?"

She put her head down. He put his hand under her chin. Her vulnerable side moved him.

"It has been a long day and not exactly the wedding day I ever pictured."

"I am sorry about that. You deserved the most extravagant wedding and if anyone saw you today, they would think that you were the most beautiful bride they have ever seen."

"Thank you for your kind words, but I don't believe in marriage."

"Why?"

"Marriage only makes people unhappy. Wouldn't you agree?"

Arius couldn't disagree with that. "Lucky we have an arrangement, not a marriage," he jeered with no reaction from Layla. "Seriously, not all marriages make you unhappy. My parents had a happy marriage."

"They are the few blessed couples. My parent's messy marriage left me motherless. My mother not only left my father, but she also disregarded what my life would be like without her."

"Why did your mother leave your father? If you don't mind me asking?"

"They were always fighting, and my father was never home. One day I came home from school and she was gone."

"How did your father react?"

"He was furious. He told me that she left him for another man. Six months later, Fiona moved in with us like my mother never existed."

"Do you think he was with your mother and Fiona at the same time?"

"I asked him, but he denied it."

"Did your mother ever contact you after she left?"

The emptiness in her eyes said more than words. "No, not even a letter. I thought she at least loved me enough to stay in touch with me."

"I could help you find her. Do you want me to find her for you?"

"It has been over ten years since I saw her. She could stay lost."

Arius thought it was best to talk about something else. "If you need anything else for your room, please let me know."

"What will your aunt think about us sleeping in separate rooms?"

"She never comes upstairs because of her bad arthritis ankles. We just need to act a little lovey-dovey around her."

"Like we did earlier. You are a good kisser for someone who hasn't been with a woman in a few years."

"You are bringing that up again. I am not wondering about your sex life."

Layla was amused by Arius' words. "So, you are wondering. I have nothing to hide."

"Maybe some things should be left hidden."

"Here is a freebie for you. The last time I've been in a relationship was six months prior to when I left Brooklyn. Next time you want to know something else about me, you will have to find out for yourself."

Now he understands what her father was talking about. "Is that a challenge, sweetheart? I am not that rusty."

Maybe, the two years weren't going to be so boring after all. Layla thought of the many ways she was going to challenge Arius. "Rusty is not a word I would ever use to describe you. Maybe more like freaky."

"I went from being a good-looking pervert to freaky. I see my sweetheart thinks highly of me."

"Did you call your ex-wife, sweetheart?" Layla inquired.

"No, I called her Babe. Why are you asking?"

"I thought you called all your wives, sweetheart," she said with a smile.

"Do you call all your boyfriends, honey?"

"No. Would you like me to call you something naughtier?" Layla found him very entertaining.

"Let's stick with honey."

The heat was definitely on.

"I need to get Darius ready for bed," Layla decided to behave.

"I could do it, if you don't mind. That will give you a chance to freshen up."

"Thank you." Freshen up for what? Layla wanted to get down and dirty. Instead, she went to the bathroom and took a nice cool shower. It gave her a chance to think about her day. She was a married woman. This was her new home with her new family. Also, with a man she was already horny for. Damn Arius for turning her into a thinker.

Layla got out of the bathroom and heard Arius singing rock-a-bye to Darius. At that moment, he was the most appealing man in the world. Arius fascinated her in ways no other man ever did. It went beyond his kindness; it was his sensitivity that seduced her without him even knowing it.

"He is dead asleep." This was the first time any man ever put Darius to sleep. He was a pro for someone who had no kids.

Arius turned around to see Layla standing in the doorway wearing an open silky pink robe revealing a lace nightgown. The temperature went up by ten degrees.

"I better put him down." Arius laid Darius down in the crib. He tucked him in and thought about how good it was to have a baby in the house. "I need to get cleaned up. Have a good night."

"Good night, honey." He left the room.

Layla never in a million years would have imagined this would be her wedding night in a room with her baby. So romantic. She should be having the best sex ever. Instead, she put the covers over her head and tried to get some sleep.

After an hour of trying to sleep with no success, Layla decided to go get another piece of cake. She opened the door and saw a dim light underneath Arius' door. Maybe he had something better than cake to help her sleep. She knocked on the door.

"Come in," Arius observed Layla scroll into his room with her racy nightgown. He laid in bed shirtless with the covers around his waist.

"I saw your light was on and thought you might still be up," she examined his muscular chest.

"Is there a problem?"

"I am having problem sleeping. I was hoping you could help me." Layla could feel his eyes burning through her nightgown.

"How can I possibly help you?"

Her nipples pierced through her nightgown. "I was hoping you could give it to me." More like cover his lips on her nipples.

A drop of sweat fell off his forehead. "Give you what?"

Her fingers innocently stroked her cleavage. "What I have been wanting from you since our bus ride." Layla studied his uneasiness with pleasure.

His eyes were being hypnotized by her fingers. "What could that be?" he mumbled.

"Don't act like you don't know what I want," her tongue licked the top of her lip.

"Stop talking in riddles and tell me what it is, so I could give it to you quickly."

His nervousness turned her on enormously. "Why are you trying to get rid of me so fast? This is our honeymoon night. I deserve more than a quickie."

"Layla, I am not in the mood. It has been a long day. We both need to get some sleep." Arius felt his heartbeat racing.

"I thought a newly married couple didn't get any sleep on their honeymoon night."

"We are not like most couples."

"You are definitely right about that," Layla decided to stop her game. "Could you please give me book three by MD?" she giggled. "What else would I want from you?"

Arius got out of bed wearing a black silky boxing short. He searched for the book in his bookcase.

"Nice boxing shorts. I figured you for a guy who slept in the nude."

He ignored her while his fingers probed for the book.

"I never pictured you for someone who hits the gym." She bit the corner of her lip.

"Here it is." He pulled the book out of the shelf and pretended to hand it to her. Before she could take it, he pulled it back. "Stop playing games with me before you get played with."

She pulled the book out of his hand. "I have played a few times before and trust me, I could keep up. Would you like to put me to the test?" her eyes dared him, but his mind tamed him.

"You better go before I make you eat your words."

She was looking forward to getting to know her newfound husband. "Have a good night, honey, and stop looking at my butt." Layla walked gradually back to her room.

Arius' eyes were glued to her butt. It was obvious she was not wearing any underwear. His body was reacting in ways that it hasn't in years. How could he get any sleep now when she just woke up a sleeping beast?

CHAPTER 7

An Awakened Beast

The beast was wide awake searching for food when Arius woke up. It has been more than three years without any reaction to any woman. He was convinced that he was impotent. Thank goodness he wasn't. Layla's childish games were to thank for that.

Arius hurried out of bed and grabbed his towel. He prayed Layla was nowhere on site. The last thing he wanted was for her to see the results of her seductive games. He opened the bathroom door and bumped into the seductress herself. She didn't look like her regular well-kept self. Arius pictured Darius was not in the bath mood this morning. Layla resembled a cute wet poodle. The wet oversized t-shirt swung to her skin revealing her full luscious breasts. Which delighted the beast.

Layla did not understand the urgency Arius was in to get into the bathroom, until the beast made a formal introduction. She was unable to take her eyes off of him.

"Good morning, I see someone is wide awake," she said, as she examined the beast struggling to come out of Arius' boxers.

He quickly covered up. "Good morning, Layla. Excuse me, I need to take a shower." He tried to go around her with no success.

"Darius wants a morning hug." Darius was hanging out of her arms anxious to be held.

Arius quickly grabbed Darius and gave him a hug. "Good morning, Darius. I hope you had a good night's sleep." Darius grabbed on his face and he gave him a kiss.

"At least, he did." Layla wanted to grab hold of the beast and give him a kiss. Arius gave her back the baby. She quickly grabbed his towel. "What's the rush?" Layla teased.

Arius snatched the towel out of her hand to cover back up. "I am in no mood for any more of your games, Layla. Now if you will excuse me, I need to take my shower."

She moved out of the way. "Make it a long cold one, honey." Arius slammed the door behind her.

The cold shower helped Arius release more than stress, it calmed the beast. He even decided to shave his fuzzy beard. It had been almost six months since he shaved. He missed seeing his smooth face. Now if only he could shave away Layla's frisky behavior.

Today getting dressed up was a harder task than usual for Arius. He has always been a well-organized guy, now he couldn't put a simple outfit together. Thoughts of Layla's seductive games consumed him.

After an hour of grappling to get ready, he was finally ready to confront Layla. He entered the kitchen to find his aunt and Layla laughing. Darius was busy playing in his highchair with his toys. If he didn't know about the arrangement, he would call it his perfect home.

"Good morning, everyone." He said as his eyes gazed at Layla. She was gussied up with her wet hair slicked back in a ponytail. Her radiance filled the whole room with her lips so inviting.

"Good morning, Arius." Aunt Brianna noticed the freshly shaved Arius. "It is good to see your sweet face again, but what's with the cranky expression the first morning as a newlywed?"

He went to pour himself some coffee and he saw a big plate of food on the counter for him.

"Honey, you look so handsome without that grizzly beard," Layla expressed.

"Thank you. So sweet of my wife to commend me," Arius replied sarcastically.

"Why are you in such a sour mood, Arius?" his aunt asked.

Arius stared at Layla.

"He is upset with me for playing a game with him last night. He didn't find it as amusing as I did." Layla winked at Arius.

"My nephew will surprise you with the number of games he knows how to play," Aunt Brianna informed Layla.

"I can't wait for him to start playing with me."

Arius listened to them discuss him while he sipped on his coffee. "I am sitting right here." He had no time for the double team that was going on. He continued to drink his coffee.

"Arius, why didn't you enjoy the game Layla was playing with you?"

He started coughing as the coffee went down the wrong pipe. Layla chuckled. Arius managed to clear his throat. "Trust me, the game was way too easy," he replied.

Layla was aroused by his shyness. "I am opened to learning more difficult games," she was stimulated.

Arius picked up his coffee and plate of food to go. "Thank you, Aunt Brianna for breakfast," he said politely.

"Layla made breakfast," his aunt stated.

He examined the plate of food. It had eggs, bacon and pancakes, and fresh fruits on it. A feast made for a king. "Thank you. I thought you had your hands full with the baby." He was impressed.

"I wanted to make my husband a special breakfast to thank him for an exhilarating night," she stroked the side of his leg.

Arius remained calm not to awake the beast. "Thank you. I have some work to do. I will eat it in my office." He gave a merry Darius a kiss and then decided to kiss Layla before leaving the room. She watched him walk away with his sexy bun.

She waited to hear Arius close his office door before she started questioning Aunt Brianna about her nephew. It was time to get some information about her husband.

"I will clean the dishes. Why don't you have a seat?" Layla insisted.

Aunt Brianna sat down. "Thank you, Layla. Ever since you came here, you have been so attentive to me. There is no need to treat me like a helpless elderly."

"You are the youngest, strongest person I know. I honestly enjoy taking care of you. I am more than capable of washing a few dishes and straightening up a bit." Layla did not want her to find out the real reason for her obliging nature.

"You need to focus your energy on little Darius and Arius. I could take care of myself, but you are very sweet in helping me out."

"We are one big family and family helps each other out," Layla wondered how to start the awkward conversation. "Can I ask you a question about Arius?"

"Sure, what is it?" Aunt Brianna had an idea what Layla wanted to know.

"Arius told me about his failed marriage. It is apparent that he was madly in love with his ex-wife," Layla paused trying to find the right words.

"You don't have to be shy around me." Darius giggled at his auntie.

"Do you think he is still in love with her?" Layla hoped she did not sound insecure.

"Why would he still be in love with someone who broke his heart?"

"Arius seems a little reserved. I have a feeling he is not ready to give me a hundred percent of himself yet."

"My nephew is a little shy. He needs time to mellow out. Trust me, he would have never married you if he was still in love with his ex-wife. I could see how much he cares about you," Aunt Brianna told her the truth.

"Arius is a good guy with a big heart. He seems to be a caring person."

"He is loving too. Arius has toughened up after his divorce, but I am starting to see the old Arius again. He is an affectionate man with a heart of gold. When he loves, he loves unconditionally. Give him some time to loosen up," Aunt Brianna suggested.

"I don't think loosen up is in Arius' vocabulary." They laughed.

"Arius is very down to earth when you get to know him. He will surprise you."

"I will wait in anticipation."

"I have one request of you." Aunt Brianna hoped Layla would not take her request in the wrong way. "Please don't hurt him. He will never recover if you take him down that dark path again."

"I respect Arius and Darius adores him. We both are hoping for the best outcome." Layla would have to cross more than her fingers to accomplish that.

"We all are," Aunt Brianna prayed silently.

The first few weeks went by very quickly as Arius stayed busy in his office. Layla got all dolled up every morning to get a reaction from him, but he was always locked up in his office. He worked the whole day and came out in the evening. He would play with Darius and put him to bed every night. The only person he had little time for was Layla and that made her furious. Getting a man's attention has never a problem for her. Until now. Why was it so hard to get

Arius' attention? Was she not his type? That was not possible. Layla was every man's type.

It made her furious being ignored by Arius. She was determined to give him a piece of her mind. Layla waited patiently for him to retire one night to express her frustration. More like, barged into Arius' room while he was undressing. He was startled when he was about to take off his pants.

"What is the problem now, Layla?" He swiftly pulled up his pants.

Seeing Arius in his underwear was a distraction for a brief moment, but Layla had to get something off her chest. "You are the problem."

Here we go again, Arius thought. "How am I the problem? I have been busy most of the day. How could I be a problem to you?"

"Well, you are. You are the meanest person I have ever met."

He thought she looked so cute blowing off steam. He bursted out laughing.

"It's not funny."

"Why am I mean?"

"You just are." How could she tell him it was because he has been ignoring her?

"I am so mean that I sat next to you on the bus keeping perverts from sitting next to you. I am so mean that I helped you out with your father and out of an arranged marriage. I am so mean that I opened my home to you and Darius without wanting anything back in return. Please tell me how I am mean?" Now he was upset because he thought he had done all the right things.

"That's for you to lose sleep trying to figure out. Have a miserable night." She stormed out of the room and slammed the door. The reaction Layla was expecting to get, she definitely got. Arius spent the whole night bewildered.

Arius woke up the next morning, more tired than rested. He managed to get a couple of hours of sleep thanks to Layla. He just couldn't understand what he did to upset her. He was determined to make it up to her by making her breakfast before he goes to his office.

By the time Layla came down with Darius, she was disappointed that Arius was not in the kitchen. She felt bad getting upset with Arius because of her selfish need for attention. With no sign of him, it only meant that he was in his office once again. She wondered if her comment had any impact on him.

"Good morning, Layla. You are downstairs later than usual. Did Arius keep you up?" Aunt Brianna was hoping for some steamy dirt from Layla. "I mean Darius."

"It was definitely Arius."

"Really." Aunt Brianna wanted to open a bottle of champagne.

"We just got into a little tiff."

Aunt Brianna's smile turned upside down. "A tiff over what?"

"I misunderstood something he did, and I called him mean."

"Why is he mean?"

"I was upset with him for spending all his time in his office. As a matter of fact, I am going to apologize to him, and it will give me a chance to check out his office." Layla checked herself out on the stainless-steel microwave door.

"He doesn't usually let anyone in his office while he works." Aunt Brianna knew exactly what she was going to check out.

"I am sure he will make a few minutes for his wife. Could you please watch Darius for me?"

"Sure, I will. I could put him in the playpen in the living room while I clean up." She looked at a stunning Layla. "You look beautiful as always."

Layla hugged her. "Thank you. I am hoping to take his attention off work for a few minutes."

"I am sure you will," Aunt Brianna smiled. Layla gradually walked towards Arius office. She got nervous as she got closer to the door.

Arius sat in his office unable to focus because of thoughts of Layla and her enticing games. He couldn't get that first night out of his mind. She looked spellbinding in her pink lace nightgown and the way her butt bounced when she left his room almost gave him a heart attack. She managed to wake up a beast that has been sleeping since the day he walked in on his ex-wife and cousin.

Every morning after that night with Layla's flirtatious game left the beast searching for her. Arius' only escape was being locked up all day in his office. He buried himself in his projects to distract his mind from thinking about Layla. Now, here he was once again lost in thoughts of her. Arius snapped out of it and picked up the phone to make a call when the pounding on the door interrupted him.

"Come in." He watched Layla walk in with her hourglass figure. His eyes were fixed on her tight Guess jeans that did her body justice.

Layla pretended to check out Arius' office that was nicely decorated with dark chocolate leather furniture and cherry wood desk. There were a couple of computers and equipment with a wall full of pictures with celebrities and awards.

Arius watched her in amusement. He wanted to ask her why she was in his office, but he decided to let play her game.

"Hi, my mean husband," she finally said.

"Hi, my livid sweetheart." He anticipated that she was up to no good.

"Compliments won't get you out of the doghouse."

"My doghouse is my office. What do I owe the honor of your visit?"

"I can't see where my husband spends all his time?"

"Are you curious to see my office or are you here to play more games with me?" Subconsciously, he would not mind the latter.

"Which game is that?" Layla approached him.

"Last night, you were furious with me. Now you want to see my office. Next thing, you will be seducing me again."

"I am still upset with you, but I would rather for us to be at peace."

Arius was perplexed. "Peace? I get the feeling you want more than peace."

Layla was intrigued by the playful Arius. "You must be in a good mood."

"It is obvious you are up to no good with your tantalizing jeans which are screaming, 'help me out of them'."

"My ravishing jeans have a mind of its own. I see it has gotten your attention."

More than his attention was gotten. "Isn't that what you were hoping for?"

"What is wrong with a woman seducing an attractive guy?" Layla was aroused.

"You finally admit you are seducing me," he applauded her.

"What if I am? I thought you would have appreciated it since you haven't been with a woman in a few years."

"I did not confide that information to you so you could keep bringing it up."

"You confided in me, so I could use the information at the appropriate time." She sat on the desk in front of him enticing an awakened beast.

"Is this the appropriate time once again since you are determined to seduce me in every room of the house."

"If I had plans to seduce you, I would have worn something much tighter."

"I don't think you could get any tighter than those jeans," he pulled on her jeans.

"Honey are you being naughty?" her devious eyes taunt him. "These jeans are worth the fight it takes to put them on." Her Guess jeans never failed her before. She got the beast stretching out.

"What do you want, Layla?" Arius wished he was a real superhero to see through her jeans.

"Sorry to disappoint you, I did not come here to seduce you." She saw a slight dispiritedness in his eyes. "I came to apologize for my behavior. To start off with, I honestly thought you would have remembered our conversation on the bus about you letting me read book three. Since that night, you have been arrogant and ignoring me for weeks."

"That is the reason why you barged into my room last night?" Arius laughed out loud. "Mark my words, I have not been ignoring you." How could he tell her that it was too distracting to be around her? "I am a busy man working on a lot of projects. I have little time to play games with you."

"I only play games with you to get your attention which you refuse to give me." Layla got straight to the point.

"My attention is on my work. Next time you want to play, please inform me first."

"I don't usually need an appointment to play with any man," she said as her tongue slid across her lips.

"Your flirtatious tongue is going to get you into trouble." The beast enjoyed her flirtatious nature.

"I am sure there are parts of you that appreciate my amorous tongue," She was definitely right about that.

"Here we go again. How could I accept your apology when you are in my office playing more games?"

"You started by asking me to inform you when I want to play. It is hard for me to back out of a naughty conversation."

"It was an innocent request. You made it into a risqué discussion." He could smell her enticing perfume. "You even put on a seductive perfume to help your game today."

"Do you like the smell of my indecent perfume? It is soft on the nose but very inviting to other parts of the body."

He knew exactly what part she was talking about. "They must have made the perfume especially for you."

"I will take that as a compliment. You have a nice office. I could see you getting a lot of work done here." Her heel went up his leg.

"Would you like to get some work done with me?" He put his hands around her ankle and lifted up her leg.

Layla started biting on her lips in anticipation. "It depends on what kind of work you are talking about."

He got up and stood in front of her. "The kind that involves me throwing you on my desk and working the hell out of you." He put her leg down. "But your jeans are beyond entry."

"I thought graphic designers have creative imaginations. Maybe you should use some of that creativity on me and release the beast within you."

"Or maybe, I should use my creativity to show you how you shouldn't play games with people. Now I have to get back to work." His words did not agree with his brain that had many ideas on how to get into her jeans. He couldn't keep his eyes off her jeans.

"Yet, your eyes are on my jeans probably trying to find a way to get into it." Layla challenged Arius. Will he stay in control or explore his wild side?

CHAPTER 8

Surrender to Lust

For once, Arius agreed with Layla and he was ready to surrender to his lustful feelings. "If I release the beast, there is no turning back."

She gave him an invitation when she opened her legs. He gradually moved between her legs. They made eye contact as the beast started to maneuver. Arius pulled her closer and Layla got ready for his creativity. His lips covered hers aggressively into a passionate kiss. Her fingers trembled as she unbuttoned his shirt. He pulled her t-shirt out of her jeans and tossed it on the floor to reveal her lacy red bra.

"Arius!" The moisture beneath her increased.

"You don't want to play?"

"Yes, I do." Her body ached for him. "I just had no idea your hands were so quick," she said, as she struggled to unbutton the last button on his shirt.

"Trust me, that is the only quick part of my body."

She started unzipping his pants. "I am too horny to think about the duration, just the freakiness of the beast is my only concern." Within seconds, his pants were on the floor.

"Let the freakiness begin."

She ran her fingers on his muscular abs. His lips kissed her neck as his hands undo her bra revealing her full luscious breasts. It did not take long for his tongue to wrap around her nipple.

"Arius," she moaned. His tongue felt so warm swaddled around her nipple. Her hand went in his boxing shorts and unleashed the beast who was completely hardened by now. His size was beyond her expectation. Arius gasped in full delight. The hunger inside of him needed to be fed. He wrestled for dear life to take her pants off. Finally, he grabbed a scissor from his draw.

"What are you doing? You can't cut up my favorite Guess jeans," Layla exclaimed.

"Next time you want to seduce me, wear a skirt with no underwear." He put the scissor down and carried her to the couch. She took off her jeans and underwear in half a second. He was hypnotized by her naked body.

"Are you going to just stare at me? The beast is waiting."

"It has been a while since I saw a woman's naked body." His eyes digested the stunning image in front of him.

"I am more focused on your very functional package." Layla pulled him on top of her. Arius was ready to enter her valuable asset when he heard a buzzing sound.

"Ignore it," she said, as she tried to guide the beast in herself.

"I have an important Facetime with Tyler Perry." Arius debated what he should do. The beast stood tall to protest, but Arius had the final word when he started getting dressed.

"The Tyler Perry?" She raced to get dressed too.

"Yes. Now you need to show yourself out, Layla." He hurried to pick up. "Good morning, Tyler. Sorry, it took so long for me to answer." Arius adjusted his collar.

"No problem. It gave me a chance to finish my breakfast, direct a movie, and use the bathroom." Tyler kidded.

Layla finished getting dressed and waited patiently to get Arius' attention. She waved her hands, but he ignored her. "Arius!" she yelled.

"Who is that?" Tyler inquired.

That was Layla's cue. She went and squeezed her big butt next to Arius. "Hi, Mr. Perry, or is it Tyler to your close friends?" Layla fixed her hair with her fingers.

"Hi, any friend of Arius could call me Tyler. Who is this Arius?" Tyler examined the awkward couple.

"This is my wife, Layla," Arius replied.

"Congratulations. I spoke to you a couple of months ago and you did not mention that you were getting married." Tyler had a puzzled look on his face.

"Thank you. We are a spontaneous couple. We met on the bus ride back to New York and fell head over heels in love." She kissed Arius on the cheek.

"What a romantic story? You should tell MD your story, Arius. I am sure she could come up with a best-selling book in a month." They all laughed.

"It is time for my wife to tend to the baby. Say goodbye, Layla." Arius lifted her off the chair.

"Baby?" Tyler asked.

"Bye, Mr. Perry. I mean Tyler. Talk again soon."

Arius helped her to the door. Before he could close the door, she blocked the door with her heel. She needed to ask him a quick question.

"Arius, when will we continue to play release the beast?"

"Layla, this is my office I work in. You are no longer allowed to come in here."

"So, we will finish the game in the bedroom?"

"Layla, we are going to have a long talk later to establish some rules." Arius continued to push her out the door with no luck.

"I think I am familiar with the rules of the game. Why do I have to wait for later? How long exactly is later? The beast needs some good food now." The more words that came out of her mouth, the crazier Arius got.

"I need to work for a few hours. Why don't you go shopping with my aunt?"

"You want me to spend Darius savings?"

He took his wallet out of his pocket and gave her his credit card. "Use my credit card. Do not spend more than five hundred dollars."

She took the card. "I can't even buy a Coach handbag for five-hundred dollars."

"Then buy me a tie."

"I had no idea you had expensive taste. I will buy you a tie and a pair of socks."

"Don't you dare buy me a tie and socks worth five hundred dollars. Give me back my card."

Layla put the card behind her back. "Seven hundred and fifty dollars and it is a deal."

"What do you need fifty dollars for?"

"Some sexy underwear." She pulled on his belt bucket. "Can I borrow your Mercedes?"

"Absolutely not! Use my aunt's minivan."

"Arius! That is the most hurtful thing you have ever said to me. I have never driven a minivan before."

"There is a first time for everything. If you go over seven hundred and fifty dollars, I will report my card stolen." Those were his last words before he closed the door and returned to Tyler.

"I am so sorry, Tyler. What were we talking about?"

"Before we start our meeting, the red lipstick looks better on your wife and you should zipper up your pants."

Arius blushed. "I will be right back." He got up to fix himself up.

"And I cannot wait to hear about this new game called release the beast." Arius was embarrassed to the max.

Aunt Brianna was making herself a cup of tea when Layla entered the kitchen. She noticed Layla's messy hair and clothes. She waited for some smutty details.

"Auntie, I should be making you some tea."

"Don't be silly, Layla. I could make my own tea." She took her cup and sat down. "I thought you got lost."

Layla smirked, "That would be better than getting kicked out of my husband's office." She searched for Darius. "Where is Darius?" she asked.

"He has been sleeping for about thirty minutes now. That was a long apology. Arius usually does not allow anyone in his office for no longer than five minutes."

"I just got banned. He was nice enough to show me an old game he had in storage for a few years."

"He must really trust you to share his game with you. Did you like playing it?"

Layla liked playing it a whole lot. "It was quite entertaining, but I did not make it to the final level. Arius got a Facetime call from Tyler Perry and had to answer it."

She could see the disappointment on Layla's face. "You could always play it later." Aunt Brianna wanted them to play more than Layla did.

"Arius is being very selfish. He doesn't want to play later. It seems like everything I say and do comes out wrong."

Aunt Brianna felt sorry for her. "Why don't you try doing the opposite of what you feel like doing? It won't hurt to try."

"Thank you for your advice. It has been a long time since I got advice from a wise woman. My mother left my father during a critical time in my life. Instead of becoming a young lady, I became a wild girl. I got into one trouble after the next. I do not blame my mother for my wild ways. I made those decisions and have to live with them."

"You are a good mother, Layla. Don't let your mother's actions define your life."

"Arius is lucky to have you."

"You have me too. He will come around. Be patient and let him lead."

That was going to be difficult for Layla to do since she has always led with her provocative ways. She did consider Aunt Brianna's advice. If she stepped back and allowed Arius to pursue her, then she would finally finish playing the game.

"Until that day comes, he gave me his credit card for us to go shopping with."

"What's the limit?"

"He said for us to shop until we drop." Aunt Brianna ran to her room to get ready.

Six hours later, Layla and Aunt Brianna returned to find Arius cooking dinner. He looked sexy with his apron on. Layla thought about their erotic morning. His gentle hands exploring her body left her with goosebumps.

Arius, on the other hand, got no work done. Thoughts of Layla's corneous behavior and voluptuous body left him stimulated the whole day.

Layla brushed against his arm and his nervousness caused him to drop the spatula on the floor.

"Sorry, honey." Layla grinned.

He avoided looking at Layla and focused on the steak.

"Thank you, Arius, for the shopping spree. Layla and I had so much fun. We brought you some chicken wings."

"You're welcome, auntie. I am glad you enjoyed yourself. I hope you brought yourself something nice, Layla." He wondered if she went over their agreed amount.

"Yes, I did. Thank you so much, honey." She gave him back his card and a hug.

It felt so good to hold her in his arms. All sense of control disappeared with one touch. "You're welcome. Anything for my sweetheart." He turned to his aunt. "I made steak and baked potatoes. Do you want some?"

"No, thank you. We are stuffed." His aunt answered.

"Where is my little man?" Darius opened his arms for Arius to pick him up. "Did you enjoy driving the minivan, sweetheart?" he asked while he picked up an anxious Darius.

"Yes, it was very enlightening." Layla sucked her teeth.

Arius wished he could have seen her.

"I bought you something." She handed him a small gift bag. He saw a pair of socks and silk tie.

"Layla, you actually bought me an expensive tie and sock."

She laughed at him. "No, silly. It was on clearance for a hundred dollars for both of them."

The relief on Arius' face was priceless. "Thank you." Darius rubbed his tired eyes as he laid his head on Arius' chest.

"I better clean up the baby and get him ready for bed."

"I could clean him up later, if you are tired from your shopping spree."

Layla took Darius from Arius. "Thank you, but I have to feed him too." She backed up before leaving the room. "Arius, I was wondering if you wanted to watch a movie later."

Arius thought about his answer carefully. He could not risk being alone with her again. "I have more work to do. Maybe another time."
Aunt Brianna could see the disappointing look on Layla's face.

"Have a good night, everyone." Layla went upstairs with Darius.

"Arius, do you realize that you hurt Layla's feelings? You are being mean."

"What are you talking about? Has everyone lost their minds here? Now you think I am mean." He put his plate down and took a seat.

Aunt Brianna pulled out a chair across him. "It is obvious you are avoiding her."

"What has Layla told you?"

"I have eyes and ears. I know everything that is happening here. Your wife is a beautiful sexy lady who is very much attracted to you."

"You do not have to tell me what my wife looks like. I have eyes and ears too since she is constantly playing games with me."

"What is wrong with playing with your wife? You are a handsome young man."

"I am exhausted by Layla's games."

"Exhausted or awakened? I see how you have changed these last few weeks."

"What are you talking about?"

"You have a thing for her. She is bringing back the man that Sierra destroyed."

"Don't be ridiculous. I barely know her."

"You knew her enough to marry her and invited her into your home. It is as if you developed feelings for her when your uncle spoke about her."

Arius could not deny it.

"Do not let your past with your ex keep you from having a happy future with someone who clearly likes you."

"We have an arrangement and that is it," Arius insisted.

"Have you forgotten; I know you like the back of my hands. You spent a year after Sierra left you locked up in this house. Then you ran down to Georgia not only to take care of your uncle but to hide from the world. Sierra went on with her life while you moped around feeling sorry for yourself. You were a good husband and family member. All that stopped after your breakup with Sierra. That was until Layla came into your life. Her presence in your life is having a positive influence on you. Please stop locking yourself in your office letting life pass you by and live a little." It hurt her to give him tough love, but he needed it.

"I know you mean well, auntie, but I am not ready to unlock my heart for anyone."

"Well, you have the next two years to get ready. Stop pushing Layla away. Even if it is for sexual reasons. Go for it. Maybe it will loosen you up for a future relationship. It is better and safer than going out there paying for it."

Arius had never heard this freaky side of his aunt. "I would never pay for sex. Anyway, why would I open myself to someone who will probably leave me when the two years are up?"

"How could you be so sure of that? What are you not telling me?"

"It's nothing. Forget I said anything. I am going to eat in my office." Arius did the walk of shame back to his office. Aunt Brianna suspected Arius was keeping something from her and Layla. Whatever it was, Arius was not ready to share that information with anyone. Especially Layla.

In the meantime, Layla felt like crying after she put Darius down to sleep. She just couldn't understand what she was doing wrong. Or was Arius waiting around for his ex to run back to him. Maybe she should throw in the towel and hoped the two years would go by quickly.

Arius sat in his office feeling bad for hurting Layla's feelings. That was not his intention. He was baffled about his feelings for someone he hardly knew. There was no doubt about the sexual chemistry they had. His only fear was he might lose control of his heart if his body gave in to her seduction. Was his aunt, right? Should he give Layla a chance or just enjoy some incredible sex with her? He sat drained in his thoughts.

An hour later, Arius knocked on Layla's door and got no reply. He turned the doorknob, but the door was locked. She must really be mad at him to lock her door. He heard some movements, but she didn't say a word.

"Layla, I could hear you. Please open the door." Arius pleaded.

"Darius is asleep," she said angrily.

"I am here to talk to you. Can we please talk for a few minutes," he begged.

"Now you have a few minutes for me. Leave me alone and go back to work."

"I am sorry, Layla. I brought you the last piece of cake as a peace offering." Arius knew Layla had a sweet tooth.

She had her eyes on that last piece of cake all morning. Layla was mad, but her stomach was always in the mood for cake. She got up and unlocked the door.

Arius came in and found Layla sitting on the bed giving him her back. He went around to place the cake on the nightstand. He sat down on the other end of the bed not knowing where to begin. "I thought you were up reading."

"I already finished reading book three the same week you gave it to me. I haven't had a chance to return it to you." She picked up the plate and began eating the cake.

"The last piece is the best tasting piece." Arius' humor needed some work.

Layla kept on eating.

"I am sorry if I hurt your feelings in any way. My aunt thinks that I was mean to you. It was not my intention. I look forward to watching a movie with you, but I have been more busy than usual."

She put the cake down and gave him her full attention.

"Okay, I have been keeping my distance." Arius finally fessed up. "It is hard for me to concentrate around you."

"Maybe I should move out, so you could focus better."

That was the last thing Arius wanted. "Layla, I don't want you to leave. I enjoy having you and Darius here. The house has life in it, and I relish in hearing your laughter."

"You have a funny way of showing it. You wake up bright and early to race to your office. You don't even have breakfast with us. When you finally come out, you eat dinner and then play with Darius for a couple of hours. You completely ignore me like I am invisible." Layla felt the tears rolling down her face.

Arius turned to hand her his handkerchief and moved closer to her. "Please don't cry. Nothing about you is invisible to me. I see all of you. Even when I am in my office, I hear all of you."

"So, why do you avoid me?"

He gazed into her cat eyes. "It has been three years since I have been close to any woman. Especially as close as I have gotten to you."

"Do you regret what happened between us earlier?" Layla prayed he would not say no.

"How could I regret something that brought me so much pleasure? You have awakened something in me that has been in a coma for three years."

"That's why you changed your seat on the bus. I hit a nerve when I asked if you were functional." Arius nodded. "I am sorry, I was just running my mouth."

"No need to apologize. My world changed after finding my ex in bed with my cousin. The last thing on my mind was being with another woman again."

"Until earlier. I got more than a reaction from you."

"A reaction I cannot deny. We both cannot deny our chemistry, but I promised you before we got married that I would not take advantage of you."

"It's not taking advantage, if both parties are in agreement. So, what is the problem?"

"I am an old-fashioned kind of guy. I don't go around jumping into bed with women I don't even know or love."

"Is it because your ex was you first?"

"Like my uncle, I was too busy with my education and work to meet anyone. Sierra was my sister's best friend. I had a crush on her, but I was a couple years older than her. I kept my feelings to myself until my sister set us up."

"Some people never get over their first love."

"I am over my ex. My only regret was not taking the time to get to know her better before we got married. We went from dating to engaged in six months. I don't want to rush my heart again "

"You don't need to put your heart into it. Just your body. People have relationships that are just sexual."

"I am not like regular people and you deserve more than a sexual relationship." He could see she was baffled. "Layla, I am talking about getting to know your inner soul."

"No one has ever been interested in knowing me in that way."

"I am someone who is interested. I see your beauty and sex appeal that most men would kill for. I want to know more about you. I want to know the inner Layla. The one that doesn't care what she looks like after bathing Darius, the one that wakes up every night at eleven o'clock happy to tend to Darius, and the person that cared for my uncle and cried for him after she found out he passed away. There are so many beautiful inner parts about you I want to explore."

Layla was touched by his comment. "How could you find out about my inner parts if you are avoiding me?"

"I promise not to avoid you anymore, if you stop playing games with me."

"How could we go about it?"

"We could take it slowly to get to know each other and establish some rules to keep us from jumping into bed too quickly."

"What kind of rules?" Layla was not against getting to know each other, but she was ready to jump into bed right this minute.

"First, I am a very busy man working on different projects. My office is for business, not pleasure. I apologize for what happened in my office earlier. I have no control over myself when you are around me in a good way. All my sense of beliefs and responsibilities goes right out the window with one stare or word from you. That has never happened to me before. I cannot allow myself to surrender to lust and make irresponsible decisions. We both need to be more mature and responsible. Do you agree with me?"

"I agree a hundred percent. Your office is for business only. I will not invade your business space again."

This has started off on a good note, Arius thought. "Second, releasing the beast game is on pause. It is obvious we are sexually attracted to each other, but I would like to get to know you better. Call me traditional if you want, but that is the way I am."

Layla thought very carefully what her response would be. "Are you saying that we are not going to continue playing?" was all she could ask.

"I said the game is on pause. That does not mean it has ended. We have both been out of commission for a while. We cannot let lust make us act like animals."

She wanted to tell him, "I like acting like an animal, and please take me right now," but she needed to do the opposite as Aunt Brianna advised her. "You are right, Arius. It has been a while since a man has kissed me the way you have or wrapped his tongue around my nipples the way you have." Arius started reacting to her sensual words. "I am only human reacting to your kiss and touch. I have been acting on my horny hormones. That was very unladylike of me. You are a gentleman and deserve to be treated like one. Not treated like a piece of meat to satisfy my cravings. I will behave myself from now on." She got up with her head down in shame. He gently took hold of her hand. "Did I say something wrong?"

He tenderly sat her back down. "Layla, no one has ever made me lose control the way you have. I like being in control of myself and my feelings."

"Playing it safe isn't going to get you nowhere in life. There is nothing wrong with losing control with the right person." Her glance sent electricity down his spine.

"I want you, Layla, but I want you in the right way. Maybe we should renegotiate our arrangement."

Did those words really come out of his mouth? She saw there was some hope after all. "What do you mean by that?" Her eyes lit up as he struggled to find the right words to say.

"I am very attracted to you and the beast has awakened. We could change our arrangement to fit our needs while we take things slowly."

"What do you mean by slowly?" At this point, Layla would accept slowly over nothing any day.

"Kissing and caressing," he suggested.

"Touching?" Her eyes opened wide.

"With limitations. We could start above the waist" Arius could sense Layla's brain working overtime.

"Will you wrap your tongue around my nipples again?" She moved closer to him.

"Layla, you are driving me crazy," Arius blushed.

"Is that a yes?"

"If you want me to." He stared at her breasts.

"I could wrap my tongue around a lot of things too. It's only fair if you could do it--"

"Don't push your luck, Layla." He gazed into her eyes and he kissed her. Arius missed the feel of her soft tender lips on his. Her hands quickly explored his lower body. "Layla, you are already breaking a rule."

"Don't blame me if the beast is up." Her hand continued to massage him.

It felt so good. It was hard for him to ask her to stop. "I will let it slide tonight only."

"If you will let that slide, then you could let this slide too." Before he could say a word, she went into forbidden territory. Arius sat back as he released three years of stored suppression.

CHAPTER 9

Taking It Slowly

It's a beautiful morning. The song that went through Layla and Arius' head after such an amazing night. They spent the night making out and getting to know each other with more actions than words.

Layla walked on cloud nine into the kitchen. She didn't even notice Aunt Brianna watching her. She was too busy reminiscing about last night. Arius' amorous words left her captivated. He was interested in her inner soul. No man has ever said those words to her before. Was Arius the guy his uncle spoke about that would come into her life to make her happy? A part of her believed he was.

Aunt Brianna said, "Good morning" for the second time trying to get Layla's attention. She decided to just wave.

"Did you say something, auntie?" Layla came back to earth.

"I said good morning twice."

"Sorry, auntie. I was listening to the birds singing." Layla put Darius in his highchair and started preparing his cereal. Aunt Brianna put a plate of eggs and bacon for her on the table.

"While you were listening to the birds singing, I made breakfast for you two late birds. Where is Arius?"

"Thank you, auntie. Everything looks delicious. I thought Arius was downstairs already." Layla sat down.

"Did I hear someone say my name?" Arius entered the kitchen. He gazed at Layla and thought about their intriguing night. "Good morning, auntie." Arius kissed her on the cheek.

"Good morning, Arius. You are up late." His aunt observed her cheery nephew.

"I overslept." He kissed a jolly Darius and then approached Layla. "Good morning, Layla." He kissed her on the lips.

Layla stroked his leg. Instantly, the beast reacted. "Good morning, honey. You look handsome today."

Arius wore a brown crew neck sweater and jeans. Not his usual tie and buttoned-down shirt. "Thank you and you look as dazzling as ever."

The fitted red sweater dress outlined all her assets. "This is just something I threw on."

"Red is definitely your color." His eyes scoped her hard. "I see you got your beauty sleep." They made eye contact and laughed at a private joke.

"I slept like a sleeping beauty." She bit her lips.

"Were you guys watching a funny movie last night? I heard some giggling," Aunt Brianna waited eagerly for a reply.

"I was tickling Arius with my--."

"Layla!" Arius turned red, as his aunt laughed.

"I didn't know my nephew was ticklish."

"There are a lot of things you do not know about Arius." Layla enjoyed taunting Arius.

"I have a busy day ahead of me. Have a nice day ladies." He hesitated before leaving the room. "Layla, would you like to watch a movie later?"

"I would love to, honey." She grabbed his arm. "Aren't you forgetting something, honey?"

Arius kissed her gently on the lips. Aunt Brianna was delighted by this new revelation. She anticipated many brighter days.

The following weeks, Layla and Arius spent renegotiating their agreement. Their exploration became very creative. Even though Arius continued to be a gentleman, the temperature inside continued to rise. They played new games and spent countless hours talking.

Arius got informed about Layla's childhood and all her likes and dislikes. Layla was also very entertained by Arius' childhood adventures with his siblings. He was very interesting for a conservative guy.

With all the information Layla gathered about Arius, she came up with a way to brighten up his afternoon and hopefully get herself unbanned from his office.

He mentioned how special he felt when his mother made him his favorite lunches and included a thoughtful note for school. Layla began preparing him her special lunches with a sensual note and placed it outside his office.

Arius always looked forward to lunchtime. One day he called Layla to his office to show her his appreciation. "Layla!" he yelled.

She ran back and opened his office door. "Did my heels make too much noise?"

"It wasn't your heels. Every day you bring me lunch and naughty notes outside my office. I wanted to tell you how much I appreciate it." He saw the spark in her eyes.

"You're welcome. I enjoy adding a little zest to your afternoon," she smiled but longed to be in his arms. "I won't keep you. I know how busy you are, and your office is for work."

He gently took her hand before she could leave. "I never forgot your first visit to my office. I miss your interruptions."

"What do you miss the most?" She moved closer to him.

"I missed seeing your sweet face and hearing your seductive voice."

"I miss you too, but I am trying to follow the rules."

His finger traced the side of her face. "I appreciate you following some of the rules. There are days I sit in my office wondering what you are doing or if you are thinking about me as much as I am thinking about you."

She kissed his finger when it reached her lips. "You are always on my mind."

He kissed her tenderly. "Maybe we can adjust the rules to fit our needs." Layla listened carefully. "I could take a lunch break to eat your delicious lunches and take some time to implement your notes with you.”

“I am no longer banned from your office." Layla embraced him in joy. "I would be delighted to have lunch with you.” Her lips found his as she pushed him on the couch.

“Sweetheart, are you being naughty again?”

“Just the way you like it.” They spent their first lunch date on the couch for an hour. If Layla had her way, she would have spent the whole day in Arius office. He probably would have let her if he didn't have to get back to work.

Aunt Brianna was not surprised by Layla's lunch break with Arius. More and more, they were looking like a real newlywed couple. She was overjoyed for them. Layla scrolled into the kitchen with a big Kool Aid smile on her face.

"Layla, have you been unbanned from Arius’ office?"

"Arius missed me too much to ban me and he can't get enough of my special lunches."

"He is turning into his old self again. Just because of you and Darius."

"He has changed our lives too. Darius sees no one else when Arius is in the room."

"Only Darius?"

Were her feelings for Arius that obvious, Layla thought? Before she could answer her, the doorbell rang.

"Are you expecting someone?" Aunt Brianna asked Layla.

"No, but I will get the door." Layla was startled by the unexpected visitor.

"Hi, Layla. I thought you would be happy to see your father."

She greeted her father and invited him in. "This is a surprise visit. How did you find out where I live?"

He handed her a package. "Chana and Lexie asked me to mail this package to you for Darius. I decided to deliver it myself and get a chance to see where you and my grandson live."

"That was thoughtful of you. Last week, I spoke to the girls and they mentioned that they bought Darius the cutest outfit. Thank you for bringing it." Layla completely forgot Aunt Brianna was in the room. "Pop, this is Arius' Aunt Brianna."

"Nice to meet you, Brianna. I am Darren Nathaniel." They shook hands.

"It is a pleasure to meet you. I heard a lot about you."

Mr. Nathaniel was not thrilled to hear that. "I could imagine what Arius has told you about me."

"Only good things." Aunt Brianna lied and promised to say a few Hail Mary's later. "Well, it was a pleasure meeting you. I have some clothes to fold in my room. I will give you two time alone." Aunt Brianna made her quick escape.

"Please have a seat, Pop."

Her father took a seat while he looked at his surroundings. "You have a beautiful home. I wasn't expecting such a big house from your husband."

"My husband's house is not why you are here. Why are you really here?"

"When are you going to stop thinking so little of me? I am your father and I worry about you."

"There is nothing to worry about. Darius and I are fine and happy "

"That's good to hear. I wanted to buy my grandson a gift, but I am catching up on my bills."

"This is about money. Are you still losing all your money in the Casino?" Layla was not stupefied.

"I have a family to provide for. I'm not about that life anymore."

"You were about it before I left. You are probably here to ask Arius for your monthly payment. I am sure he has every intention of making every payment."

"The payment?" The light bulb turned on in her father's head. "I didn't want to tell you what Arius and I agreed on. That is men's business."

"Arius told me everything. If he missed a payment, it is because he has been very busy with many projects. He will give you your money when he gets a chance," Layla explained to her father.

"Of course, he will. Honestly, I came here to see you. I miss you, Layla." His eyes fell to the floor indicating he was lying.

"I was away for two years and you didn't miss me. I will go and ask Arius for your money?" She got up abruptly.

"Layla, let me speak to your husband privately. I am sure Arius forgot his payment because he cannot get enough of his beautiful wife."

"Let me show you to his office." Layla's father followed her down the hallway. She knocked on the door.

"I thought lunch was over with." Arius said as he opened the door. He was bewildered to see Layla's father standing behind her. "What are you doing here?"

"My father came to drop a package for Darius from my sisters." Layla said.

"I also came to see my daughter and grandson. Who I have yet to see," he snapped at Arius.

Layla did not appreciate her father's tone towards Arius. "Pop, there will be no arguing today." She turned to Arius, "My father needs to speak to you about the monthly payment."

"What!" Arius wanted to strangle her father.

"It must be a misunderstanding. Have you mailed the check out already, Arius?"

"Let me talk to your father to clear up this misunderstanding." He kissed Layla on the cheek.

She didn't want to leave them alone, but Darius woke up from his nap. "I need to feed the baby. I will be right back." Layla ran to tend to Darius.

"Come in and have a seat." Arius took a seat.

"I see you are taking good care of my daughter. I didn't expect it to last a month."

"We both know you are not here to make small talk. Apparently, you are here for more money after I paid Layla's debt in full."

"My daughter seems to think you owe me a payment. You neglect to tell her that you paid me double her debt. Why is that?" Mr. Nathaniel fished for information.

"Unlike you, Layla would have never let me pay her complete debt. I understood there must have been interest in it, so I paid you more than needed. Layla is too proud to allow me to pay you that much money and she would have agreed to your sick marriage arrangement. That is why I paid you double to leave her alone."

"Or you wanted her for your own sick selfish reasons. How would she feel about your deception?" He threatened Arius.

"Are you here to blackmail me?" Arius was fuming at this point.

"Me, blackmail my son-in-law? That is putting it harshly. You want to deceive my daughter and I want to protect her heart. I should at least get compensated for my loyalty." Mr. Nathaniel grinned.

"You give a bad name to fathers. I am glad I took Layla out of your house." Arius loathed him more than the first time he met him.

"You could take her across the world, and she will still find her way back to me. Now the big question is, are you willing to test a few weeks of pleasurable marriage life on your deception?"

Arius understood he had more to lose than him. He took out his checkbook and wrote him a five thousand dollars check. "This is the last check I will give you. Next time you ask me for money, I will tell Layla the truth." He gave the check to him.

Mr. Nathaniel was very happy with the outcome of their discussion. "What could you possibly be keeping from my daughter? Why did you really help her?"

Her father was the last person he would ever reveal that information to. "Get out of my house before I throw you out." Arius got up to escort him out.

"This is also my daughter's house and I will always be welcomed here!" Mr. Nathaniel screamed.

Layla stormed back into the room. "Pop, why are you yelling at Arius?" Layla demanded.

"Your husband told me to get out of his house. I was reminding him that it is your house too or am I mistaken."

"This has been Layla's house from the first day she stepped foot in it." Arius replied.

"Darius and I have appreciated the hospitality Arius have shown us."

"Then I am welcome too. I am your father and I need to develop a relationship with my grandson who you neglect to give him my name."

Both Layla and Arius were stunned.

"Is his middle name Darren at least?" He asked to further insult Layla.

"His middle name is Arius," Arius answered. Layla smiled at him.

"How convenient for you." her father said with a smirk.

"Arius, did you clear the misunderstanding?"

The tension veins covered Arius' forehead. "Everything is fine. It was my mistake, I thought I mailed the check out last week."

"It's not a problem." She focused on her father. "Arius would never go back on his word. You shouldn't have doubted him." Layla defended Arius.

"I see you are quick to trust. Remember what happened in your last relationship." Arius wondered what that meant. "I guess she hasn't told you all about her wild past."

"Are you here to start trouble for us, Pop?"

"Nonsense, I better get going. I want to give my grandson a hug before I leave."

"He is in the living room with his aunt." Her father left the room.

"I am sorry, Arius. This is all my fault. I was thinking about pursuing the case against the clinic. This way I can pay you and my father back."

Arius embraced her. "There will be no need for that. I could handle your father. All you need to focus on is taking care of Darius and keep being amazing to me."

"I could do that." Layla kissed all his frustration away.

"I relish in what we have." He held her tight.

"Ooh, Arius." Layla pushed him back on the couch. She was able to show him just how amazing she was.

Neither Layla nor Arius forgot her father's visit. They just decided to put it behind them and concentrate on building their relationship. Arius got a chance to learn so much about Layla when she wasn't playing games. Her father was right about her being smart. She displayed her intelligence by helping him when he got stuck on a project. Layla appreciated Arius complimenting her work. This was the first time any man saw her for more than a trophy.

Letting Arius take the lead not only helped him to feel more secure in himself, it also helped Layla to see her worth. He made her feel special, but that did not stop Layla from breaking a rule or two at times. Arius welcomed it. There was never a dull moment with her. They grew closer and Layla worked hard to get them to the final level of the game.

With Arius finding it harder to take things slowly, he took more cold showers during the day. That only indicated to him that it was time for the game to go to the last stage. He wanted their first time together to be memorable. An idea popped up in his mind, he was certain would blow Layla away. He started making a couple of calls to finalize their romantic night.

Layla was disappointed when Arius told her that he was too busy to have lunch with her. That only meant he was planning something special for them. Every week they had a date night. Sometimes they went out to an elegant restaurant, other nights they cooked a romantic dinner for each other. Her mind scrambled on how to set the mood tonight. Before she could come up with an idea, she got an unforeseen call from her best friend, Gurdie. She was beyond excited to share the news with Arius. Layla knocked impatiently on his office door.

"Come in, Layla."

"I know you said that you were busy, but I have some good news to share with you." She sat on his lap.

"I have a few minutes to hear your good news." He kissed her neck and made her giggle.

"Guess who just called me?"

"Who?" He could see the excitement in her eyes.

"Gurdie."

"Who is Gurdie?"

"Her name is Gurdine, but I call her Gurdie. She has been my best friend since high school. She called my father's house phone, and he gave her my new cell phone number." Layla beamed as she spoke about her best friend.

"You must have been excited to hear from her."

"I was. We lost contact after I left New York. She wants to pick me up around seven so we can catch up. She lives in Queens. I told her I need to be home by ten. Do you mind if I go out for a couple of hours?"

He thought it was thoughtful of her to ask. "Why would I? I am glad your best friend got in touch with you."

"Tonight, is supposed to be our quality time. I was thinking about something really romantic to top last weekend's date."

"We could have our quality time when you get back home."

"You are so sweet and understanding. It is so strange, Gurdie and I used to go out all the time. Now, I feel sad leaving Darius even for a couple of hours."

"He will be fine. There is nothing wrong with you spending time with your friend. Plus, Darius is used to me and his aunt."

Layla gave him a big kiss of appreciation. "Thank you, honey. I better let you get back to work unless you have a few minutes for your wife."

His hand traveled up her skirt. What he discovered made his day. "I have more than a few minutes." He put her on top of his desk and lifted her skirt up all the way.

"I see you implemented my suggestion."

Layla could feel the breeze between her legs. "Honey, are you breaking the rules?" She was shocked after weeks of Arius following the rules.

"I said no touching, I didn't say anything about licking." He put his head between her legs and sniffed her sweet exotic scent. Her fingers ran through his hair. One of the long anticipation Layla has been waiting for has arrived. She felt his warm tongue licking her sensuous flesh.

"Arius, ummmm..." Layla spent forty-five minutes experiencing the most unbelievable pleasure she has ever experienced. Her legs felt like spaghetti when she left Arius's office. She wondered what else Arius had installed for her.

CHAPTER 10

An Evening to Remember

Layla came down wearing a tan color turtleneck sweater and brown checked knee-high skirt. She wore her hair in a ponytail. It wasn't her usual sexy self, but her full breast took the turtleneck sweater to sexy librarian look.

Arius was playing with Darius on the couch when she entered the room. He lost all focus as his eyes followed her every move. "Darius, mommy looks so pretty."

She joined them. "Thank you, honey." She kissed Darius then Arius. "I had a great time earlier. I can't wait for later."

"Tonight is going to be an evening to remember. I promise you."

She questioned herself if she heard correctly. "Arius, are you saying what I think you are saying?"

Arius loved seeing her eyes dancing with enthusiasm. "We are ready to finish the game."

She embraced him as those words echoed in her ears. Her eyes got teary.

"Layla, what's wrong?"

"Every moment with you has been memorable in more ways than you know."

"You are very special to me." Arius was about to kiss her when the doorbell rang.

"It's Gurdie!" Layla jumped with agitation. She ran to open the door.

The two ladies screamed and did a dance of celebration. Gurdie was nothing like her name. She had an ebony complexion and long locks. Her face resembled Naomi Campbell. The only difference was her shorter height.

"Come in, Gurdie. It is so good to see you. I have missed you." They hugged again.

"Look at you." Her friend was amazed by her transformation. "You are beautiful as always with extra breasts."

"The benefits of breastfeeding."

"Are you still breastfeeding?"

"I only pump now. Darius is teething and I could feel his teeth coming in."

"That must have been painful." Gurdie examined her friend. "You look the same but in a mature conservative way."

"You haven't changed one bit. You are still my beautiful and very funny best friend. Let me introduce you to my handsome husband." Arius got up with Darius.

"Honey, this is Gurdie."

He shook her hand. "Nice to meet you, Gurdie. Layla has told me so much about you."

"I hope not everything. We were crazy back in the days."

Layla hoped Gurdie would not bring up their past. "Gurdie, this is Darius."

"He is adorable, and I see a pinch of your father. Till this day, your father terrifies me." Everyone nodded in agreement.

"You are not the only one," Layla chuckled. "We are going to be laughing all night long. This is going to be an evening to remember."

"You better finish getting ready so you could get back home by eleven."

"I said ten and I am ready."

Gurdie did not hide her disappointment on her face. "That's what you are wearing? Stop kidding me."

Arius had an uneasy feeling about Gurdie.

"What happened to my sexy friend?"

"My wife is very sexy."

Layla smiled at her supportive husband.

"He is a keeper, not like that loser Dexter. He was even asking my husband for you."

Dexter was the last person Layla wanted to talk about. "Let me get my jacket." Darius started fussing while she put her jacket on. "Boohbah, I will be right back." She felt guilty about going out.

"He will be fine. Have a good time."

"I can't wait for our quality time later." Layla whispered in his ears and then kissed both of her special guys. She glanced at her perfect new life before leaving. She finally had it all.

Gurdie took Layla to the best Haitian restaurant in Long Island, called Gou Tropikal. The restaurant made you feel like you were in Haiti with its beautiful artworks and decorations. The waitresses were dressed in Haitian vintage attires to complete the cultural presentation. Gurdie knew the owner, so they got the best table in the house.

"What are you eating?" Gurdie looked at the menu.

"Everything, plus a giant piece of pineapple upside cake." Layla always liked to eat the finest Haitian cuisine.

"I am looking at you and still can't believe it is you. Don't get me wrong you are still beautiful, but you have definitely changed."

Layla was flattered. "Thank you. Georgia matured me in more ways than one. I am sorry I lost touch with you. I was going through a lot before and after I left home."

"I understand. You didn't have to shut me out after your breakup with Dexter."

"I don't want to talk about that bum."

"You are right. He is not worth it." Gurdie could see the topic of Dexter agitated Layla. "Let's talk about the mistake the fertility clinic made. You should have sued them."

Layla had told Gurdie all the details about her stay in Georgia. "What time or money do I have?"

"I am sure your new husband has money." Gurdie unceasingly gave Layla the push she needed when she had to make a decision.

"Arius has already done enough for me. I still do not know how much money he gave my father. It could have been his whole savings."

"It was not his whole savings I am sure if you ask him, he will give it to you."

"I am not going to ask him. Arius barely knew me and helped me out. He had no expectations of me. I even tried to seduce him with no success. He was more interested in getting to know my inner soul."

"That is beyond romantic. Layla, anyone can see he is in love with you. This is the kind of love you have always talked about finding."

"I don't have a good history with love. Plus, Arius said that he is not giving his heart away easily again."

"He will in time. I could see how much he adores you."

"Adoring me, does not mean he will fall in love with me. Arius is protecting his heart. He is not ready to trust any woman again. Especially a wild woman like me."

"Are you serious, Layla? Any man would be happy to have you for a wife. Arius knows it. You are wife material." Gurdie will forevermore be her cheerleader.

"This arrangement is for two years. We never discussed staying in the marriage."

"What do you need to discuss? If you two are happy and in love, then the arrangement will dissolve, and your marriage will become permanent."

Layla wanted to believe in the best outcome too. "You always had a way of seeing the bright side of things. Thank you, Gurdie. I missed having you in my life."

Gurdie held her hand. "We are not getting separated again. We are going to see much more of each other, and I want little Najeeba to know her auntie. She is going to be three next month."

"We will have a playdate. Listen to us talking about playdates. Remember when we used to talk about what outfits we were going to wear to the club. Did we get old overnight?" Layla laughed.

"You got old. I am preserving my years. Now tell me about the beast." Gurdie was curious.

"I am not telling you any more information about the beast. Tonight, the beast and I are going to become good friends." Layla did a happy dance.

"I feel sorry for Arius. He does not know what he got himself into."

"Please do not mention the beast again. I am already moist."

"You are nasty." Gurdie heard enough about the beast. "Do you remember my Aunt Sophie?"

"Yes, how is she doing? She was always so nice to me."

"My aunt and her husband are celebrating their fiftieth wedding anniversary tonight. Her kids are throwing her a small party. Let's check it out after we eat. She would love to see you."

"Sure, but I need to get home by 10:30 the latest."

"Here we go with the curfew again. It is Saturday night. You will not be late for your appointment with the beast tonight."

Layla threw her napkin at her. She was thrilled to be back in New York around her family and friends. Her life felt complete.

The hours went by swiftly as the best friends went down memory lane. After dinner, they went to Gurdie's aunt's anniversary party. Layla was not expecting such a big party with over a hundred people. It's been a while since she has been to a big house party.

What started out as an innocent evening, was now a nightmare for Layla. She was freaking out. Not only was it after midnight, but she was still unable to find her jacket and purse. She had a bad feeling about going to the party with Gurdie. She regretted ever leaving her house. This was a disastrous evening.

Gurdie finally came back with her jacket. "Is this your jacket?"

Layla examined it. "Yes, it is, but my purse is gone." She had put her purse in the sleeve of her jacket. "Here is my phone, but it was in my Gucci purse. They stole it and they were generous enough to put my phone in my pocket." She saw all the missed calls and messages from Arius. She became tearful.

"Layla, please don't cry. He will understand."

"We were supposed to have a special night. I also missed Darius's eleven o'clock wake up. I usually rock him back to sleep. All because someone decides to steal my purse and throw my jacket God knows where. I am not too old to kick someone's butt." Layla put up her fist.

"I will get to the bottom of this when the party ends. I could call Arius and explain what happened."

"This is my problem. I should have never come here. I know my life seems boring to you, but I am happy. Arius is special to me and he cares about Darius."

"I am happy for you, Layla. We had our fun back in the days and now we are wives and mothers.

My life is not that exciting, but I would not trade it for anything in the world."

"I really enjoyed spending time with you, Gurdie. You will always be my best friend no matter where we are in life."

"Remember we promised to always be friends." They hugged. "Let me find someone to drive you home."

"You don't need to get me a ride. Everyone is having a good time. I will call for a ride." Layla made the only call she could make.

"Hi, can you please pick me up."

Arius came to pick her up without saying a word to her. Layla has never seen him so mad that he would be speechless.

By the time they got home, Layla tried to explain herself, but Arius had a few choice words for her. "How could you be so irresponsible? You said that you were going out to catch up with your friend and you ended up at a house party." Arius was furious.

"I know it looks bad, but please let me explain." She could see how hurt he was.

"It is self-explanatory. You are a mother and wife now. Your priorities should be your baby and marriage; not living the wildlife with your wing girl."

"You know I am not about that life anymore. How could you even say such a cruel thing."

"I am being cruel? Your son woke up crying for you. I had to put him back to sleep. My aunt and I are not here to babysit your child while you go and hang out. Darius is not our responsibility." Arius heard those ugly words that came out of his mouth and regretted it instantly. He saw his words cut her deep. "I didn't mean to say that." He wished he could take back.

She took a few deep breaths before replying to him, "My mother taught me a long time ago, what a person says when they are mad, it is coming from their heart. Since you said everything you wanted to say, now it is my turn." She took her jacket off and threw it on the floor. "This jacket has caused all this drama. Gurdie and I finished catching up at 9:30, I was ready to go home when she told me they were having a party for her aunt's anniversary. I went to say hi. I had no idea it was a big house party. After an hour, I was ready to go, but I could not find my jacket. Gurdie and I spent nearly two hours looking for it. When she finally found it, my purse had been stolen. The thief was kind enough to put my phone in the pocket of my jacket. I was so upset, especially after seeing all your missed texts and calls. The last thing I ever wanted to do was ruin our special night." Layla stopped to pacify herself.

Arius was at a loss for words. He felt numbed after everything he said to her.

She felt her picture-perfect life had been taken away from her. "Gurdie saw how devastated I was and offered me a ride. I clearly saw everyone had been drinking. I did the responsible thing and called you to pick me up. Now about Darius not being your responsibility, I never said he was yours or your aunt's responsibility to take care of him. He is my child and my responsibility. I just thought you cared about him enough to do so. I will never ask you to do anything for my child again." She picked up her jacket and left the room.

"Layla, come back!" he screamed after her. His aunt came out of her room.

"Why would you say such a hurtful thing to her?"

"I didn't mean it. I have been worrying about her all night long."

"Sierra has done far worse to you and you have never raised your voice at her or say such hurtful words to her."

"I care about Darius and Layla. I swear to you, auntie that I did not mean what I said." He sat on the couch as the tears came out. Aunt Brianna didn't know who to feel sorry for more. She just comforted Arius.

The night went by slower than a turtle with Layla in misery. She laid in bed thinking about her horrible night. It didn't help with Darius crying half the night because he was teething. Even if he wasn't up, she would have been up feeling miserable. Arius hurt her deeply when he said that Darius was not his responsibility. She thought he cared about Darius. Why would he say such hurtful things to her? Yes, she was wrong for staying out late, but it was not her fault. The whole day she anticipated her special night with Arius. Instead of having a passionate night, she spent the whole night crying with Darius

Arius tossed and turned the whole night wondering how to make amends with Layla. He felt bad for letting his insecurities get the best of him. He assumed she was out having fun and hooking up with other men. He was so wrong.

He woke up early and decided to make Layla her favorite breakfast. Arius brought it upstairs for her, but her door was locked. He knocked on the door.

"Layla, I have your breakfast for you." She said nothing. "I am so sorry for everything I said to you last night. Can we please talk?"

"Leave me alone. I do not want your breakfast or to talk to you." Her words went right to his heart.

"I will leave you alone. You do not need to talk to me, just eat your breakfast. I made cornmeal and spinach with avocado. If you need me to take Darius for you while you get some sleep, I could do so."

She wanted nothing to do with him. He did not care about Darius or her. "I don't need you to do anything for Darius. We are fine."

"I heard him crying all night. You must be tired. At least, bring him down to stay with auntie."

"He is just teething. Leave us alone."

Every attempt to make things right, she closed the door on him. "Ok, I will. I am leaving your breakfast by the door. Please eat." He left her breakfast and went back downstairs.

Layla swallowed her pride and took the tray of food. She was too hungry to take a stand. Arius was relieved when he heard her take the food. His aunt wanted to check in on her, but her ankles could not take the stairs.

"How is Layla doing?" his aunt asked him.

"She is not talking to me. Honestly, I do not blame her."

"Just give her some time. She will forgive you."

"I have to leave later this afternoon for my business trip. That should give her some space."

"When will you be back?"

"Monday evening or Tuesday morning. It is a one-day trip, but I can extend my trip if Layla needs me to stay away from her."

"Arius, you are not going to run away from your problems again. You are going to return when your business is done. The last couple of months, I have seen you two get closer. I haven't seen you this happy in years."

"I messed it up. I should have known something must have happened to keep her from getting home. We made some special plans, and we were both looking forward to our night together."

"There will be many more nights. Everything is going to be alright, Arius. By the time you come back, Layla will be missing you. She can't get enough of you." It was hard for Aunt Brianna to see her nephew so gloomy.

"I better start packing. My taxi is coming at four o'clock." He went back upstairs and stood by Layla's door hoping she would open it. He heard her crying like a wounded child. What he wouldn't do to hold her in his arms again? He decided to leave her alone and get ready for his trip.

The taxi arrived a few minutes before four. Arius knocked on Layla's door to inform her that he was leaving. At first, she said nothing, and then she told him bye.

"Please call me if you or Darius need anything."

"We won't need anything from you." She lied to him. She needed him to make her feel better again.

"I will miss you. Have a good night."

"I won't." If she was trying to hurt him back, she succeeded. He left wearing his heart on his sleeve.

CHAPTER 11

He is my responsibility

Layla was right about not having a good night. Darius would not stop crying. He was beyond cranky. She tried everything to comfort him. She gave him some baby Tylenol and a cool alcohol bath to soothe him, but he continued to fuss. He was burning up with a fever and he was not his usual active self. Aunt Brianna took his temperature, and it was 102. She recommended that Layla take Darius to the emergency. Fear consumed Layla as she took a cab to the hospital.

The doctor examined Darius and admitted him. The reason the medicine did not bring down his fever was because he had a bad ear infection. Layla called Aunt Brianna to inform her that Darius would be spending the night at the hospital. She insisted on her not to call Arius. Aunt Brianna disregarded Layla's wish and called Arius.

Darius finally got some sleep after the doctor gave him some antibiotics. Layla kept her eyes open the whole night to make sure he was alright. She was terrified of losing her baby.

As the sun rises, Layla's eyes burnt from lack of sleep. It had been two nights since she got any sleep. Just as she started dozing off, she heard a loud noise outside the door. Someone was arguing with the nurse.

The door popped open. "My wife needs me." It was Arius. He stared at her fatigued face. He wanted so much to hold her in his arms.

"Do you know this man, Ms. Nathaniel?"

"Ms. Nathaniel? Layla, you are my wife."

Layla had used her maiden name out of anger. "He is my husband." She could see Arius was as drained as her.

"I am sorry. We need to be very careful who goes in and out of the rooms. The doctor will be in shortly to check the baby." the nurse informed them.

"Thank you." Arius came into the room. He kept his distance.

Layla looked so distorted. Her hair was a mess and her eyes red from crying.

"Why didn't you call me, Layla?"

"Darius is not your responsibility." She turned around so he would not see the tears that rivered down her face.

"He is my responsibility. Darius has been my responsibility since I took you from your father's house."

"You told me he wasn't." She wiped her eyes with her sleeve.

"I am sorry, sweetheart. I was worried about you."

"Don't call me that. You hurt me. All I wanted to do was get back home to you and Darius. The more time I spent looking for my jacket, the more I felt our special night slipping away. That night meant everything to me.”

“I thought about the memorable night we were going to have. I covered the bed with rose petals and bought your favorite Moscato wine. I wanted our night to be perfect. When you did not show up by eleven, I had a feeling something was wrong. Then I started to worry. I left you numerous texts and messages. You cannot imagine how relieved I was to hear your voice. After I got to the address you gave me, I thought you were just partying while I was worried about you. I cannot take back what came out of my mouth, but I can beg you for your forgiveness.”

“I almost lost my baby. I didn’t even know what was wrong with my own baby. I thought he was teething, but he had a bad ear infection. What kind of mother am I? You were right, I am not responsible.” Layla started sobbing. He went to her and wrapped his arms around her.

“Layla, you are a new mother. You are learning as you go. Darius is such a happy baby and how about that big smile he gives to everyone. That smile is because you are a great mother and give him so much love. From the first day I met you on the bus, I could see how nurturing you were with him. Please do not doubt how responsible you are when it comes to him.”

“He doesn’t even have a doctor or health insurance. How responsible is that?”

“Darius has had health insurance since we got married.”

“What are you talking about?”

"I added you and Darius on my health plan after we got married. The cards came in last week."

"You did that for us?"

"I am responsible for my wife and son. If you don't mind me calling him my son."

"Your son? You consider him to be your son?"

"How could I not consider that beautiful baby to be my son?"

She laid her head on his shoulder. "Thank you for coming back to us. I needed you so much."

"Aunt Brianna called me when my plane landed. I would have been here sooner, but I had to wait for a seat on the next flight. The only flight they had made two stops. I had no choice but to take it. I needed to be here for you and Darius."

"I was so scared. He laid so motionless."

He stroked her hair off her face. "I am here now, and our son is going to be alright." His words of reassurance comfort her. He cupped her face and kissed her gently.

The doctor walked into the room to find the newlyweds sharing a tender kiss. "Excuse me," the Doctor attempted to get their attention. "Hi, I am here to check little Darius."

"Doctor, this is my husband Arius, Darius' father," Layla proudly said. "Honey, this is Dr. Brutus." They shook hands.

"We are so happy to see you. Your wife needs your support. We kept Darius overnight because his fever was high, and he was a little dehydrated. We started him on antibiotics and some fluids. I am going to check his temperature now to see if the antibiotic is working." They stepped back as the doctor examined

Darius. She was thrilled to inform them that his fever had broken, and the medicine was working. They were so excited about the good news.

Later that evening they brought Darius home. He was happy to be in his own bed again. Layla and Arius took a much-needed shower and ate some good food aunt Brianna had made them. They were both exhausted by the end of the night.

"Arius, you should get some sleep. You were up all night long at the airport."

"Layla, you were up all night long with Darius at the hospital. I could sit on the chair to keep an eye on him."

"If you are going to stay here tonight, we can share the bed. I won't bite."

"Maybe I will," he laughed. "I am just kidding. I will read my book." He got in bed next to her.

"What are you reading?" Layla's devious mind started to unravel.

"A murder mystery."

"I thought it was an erotica novel." She appeared disgruntled. "Do you mind if I read along with you?"

"You don't seem too excited."

"Being here with you is all that matters." Layla sat real close to him. As he read, her nipple rubbed against his arm. It drove him crazy. He stopped reading and closed the book

"I haven't finished reading yet."

"No more reading for the night." He got up to keep the beast tamed.

Layla was perplexed. "Was I breathing too hard on you?"

"No. Your nipple rubbing on my arm was driving me insane." Her seductive eyes told him what was on her mind. "I thought you were tired."

"When are we going to have our special night?"

"Both of us are exhausted, sweetheart. How will it be a special night?"

"I am never too tired for you. I want you, Arius." She took her nightgown off and threw it on the floor. He was hypnotized by her nakedness.

"Are you sure? I do not want to be rated for bad tired sex."

"We can skip the foul play and use our energy on the actual deed."

Arius liked her idea. He took off his pajama pants. The beast was ready.

"I had to make a case when you were ready to go."

"Your nipples can be very persuasive."

Layla opened her arms. "Come to me, honey."

He cuddled up on her silky skin. "I have missed you."

"Show me." She whispered in his ear. His lips kissed her so passionately. Their bodies rubbed together to bring the best to his peak. Arius teased her by poking the entrance of her valuable asset. She groaned like a savage beast.

"Arius, that feels so good."

"It is about to feel great." He finally entered her. Their eyes agreed it was beyond great. He felt the warmest of her asset. Each stroke, he had to restrain from coming too fast. The feeling was so intense. Her eyes rolled over from the sensation. She assisted him by putting some hip movements into it. Those belly dancing classes she took years ago, elevated the moment. Arius cursed himself for waiting so long to sample her bucket of honey. The beast was gratified as he swam in her tunnel. His strokes intensified, making her body tremble as she released her love juice. Arius was unable to hold back and his explosion followed soon after hers. He kissed her with humongous satisfaction.

"I hope it wasn't too fast."

"It was perfect." She kissed his cheek and then put her head on his chest. "Let's get some sleep. First one up, gets to wake up the other for round two."

"Deal." They fell asleep in each other's arms. Both exhausted but were fulfilled from their intimate connection.

A few hours later, Arius heard the word that brought joy to his ears. "dada." He saw Darius laying down staring at him. He got up and snuggled with him. This was his son who was indeed his responsibility. He always dreamt of having a son and now it was a reality. It brought him so much joy to do his daddy duties until Darius fell back to sleep.

Arius observed the person that made it all possible. Layla slept peacefully with her messy hair covering her face. He debated whether or not to wake her up as they had spoken about. He pulled the sheet off her naked body. She was laying on her back and her legs were apart. He accepted her invitation and decided to wake her up the best way he knew how to.

He started kissing her inner thighs. She reacted with a soft squeal of delight.

"Ooooh, ahhhh." Her upper body twisted like a snake. As his warm tongue reached her valuable asset, her body flickered. His tongue traced her asset like a pencil on a blueprint. Layla opened her eyes in contentment when she realized it wasn't a dream. She began to stroke his hair. He lifted his head up and they both realized it was time for round two. This time their bodies were re-energized.

The next following weeks for Layla and Arius were beyond incredible. They got their energy back to prolong their lovemaking. Layla's freakiness spread to Arius whose level of creativity astonished her. They blessed every room with their creativity, except Aunt Brianna's room.

As the temperature continued to cool down, their passion heated up. Arius' office was the daytime spot for their lovemaking. Layla brought him lunch every day and he gave her a generous tip. Once a week, they maintained their date night to get to know each other on a deeper level. It gave Arius a great idea for an early Christmas present. He hired some workers to renovate his basement. He was certain that Layla would love the surprise. Only if he could keep her from finding out what he was up to.

"Why can't I go downstairs, Arius?" Layla turned the lock doorknob.

"Layla, I told you that it is dangerous downstairs. They are renovating the basement to extend my workspace."

"Are you putting a bedroom downstairs?" Her face lit up by the thought.

"Like we need another bedroom to get freaky in. My business is growing, and I need the extra space."

"That's boring. I am going to watch tv with auntie."

He put his hand around her waist. "I wanted to talk to you in my office."

"Again. We did it two times already for the day if you count the shower."

"Not that. Come in so we could talk." He sat down and Layla sat down on his lap. "You sitting on my lap is very distracting."

"That's where I always sit, but if you want me to sit on the chair I will." She attempted to get up and he pulled her back down.

"I like you sitting on my lap." He kissed her cheek. "I wanted to tell you how happy you have made me since you came into my life. It's not just because of our intimate relationship. You and Darius have brought me to a brighter place in my life. I was so ecstatic a couple of weeks ago when Darius started calling me 'dada'. It brought so much joy to my heart. I know we agreed on staying married for two years and maybe it is too soon to talk about this, but I want our marriage to last for as long as possible."

She understood what he was trying to say, but he didn't mention that he loved her. "I want the same thing too, but I know you are not ready to give your heart to anyone. Could you be in a marriage without love?"

"I care deeply about you. Hopefully, in time, we can both grow to love each other."

Layla feared she had already grown to love Arius. She suspected it was best to keep that information to herself. "Anything is possible. We have plenty of time to fall in love, but I know you do want children."

"We have Darius. He will always be our first child. As you said when we first met, I could adopt a child when the right person comes along. How do you feel if we adopt?"

"You think I am the right person?"

Arius opened his mouth to answer her but was interrupted by a knock on his door.

"Arius, Layla, you have company," Aunt Brianna announced.

They wondered who it could be. When they got to the living room, there was a couple waiting for them. The lady resembled Arius with the same beautiful complexion and eyes. Her hair was thick, and naturally wavy. She was tall and had legs for days. Her eyes studied Layla like she was the encyclopedia. The guy was a good-looking conservative guy. He was envious of Arius with such a beautiful sexy lady. Arius went and greeted them.

"Layla, this is my little sister Lynn and her husband Edgar." Layla shook their hands. "Lynn and Edgar, this is Layla, my beautiful wife."

Layla noticed how cold his sister was towards her.

"Nice to meet you," they said.

"It is a pleasure to finally meet you, Lynn." Layla anticipated an exciting evening.

"Let's have a seat," Arius suggested.

Lynn and Edgar sat in the middle of the sectional. Arius and Layla sat across them on the other end.

"This is a surprise, Lynn. I haven't seen you in a couple of years," Arius inquired.

"With two kids under four, I am always busy. I still can't believe you missed your niece's baptism last year," Lynn responded.

"Uncle Darius needed me. I still can't believe you did not come to the funeral."

"I have two young kids. I sent flowers. Are you going to beat me up about it every time we talk? I am sorry."

"Lynn, your brother understands. We came here to congratulate the happy couple." Edgar became the voice of reason.

"Thank you, Edgar. My wife and I appreciate it."

"Why did I have to hear from the grapevine about your marriage? We are a family." Layla rolled her eyes up. "Did I say something wrong?"

"There is family and then there is family." Layla was not holding her tongue.

"What does that mean?" Lynn was not expecting an argument, but she was ready.

"That means, Arius is your family, and you turned your back on him when he needed your support."

"What do you know about the support I gave my brother? Arius, what have you told your supposed wife?" Lynn demanded.

"What do you mean by that? Please show my wife some respect."

Layla was cheery that Arius stood up for her.

"You were the one that turned your back on us. You left town and did not stay in touch with anyone."

"Why would he stay in touch with people who would welcome his adulterous wife and disregard his feelings?"

Aunt Brianna wanted to kiss Layla.

"I have been friends with Sierra most of my life. Was I supposed to end my friendship with her?"

"Yes, you were. She broke your brother's heart. How can you laugh with someone who brought tears to your brother's eyes?"

Lynn felt stupid. "I love my brother. That is why I am here."

"You are here to check out your brother's gorgeous new wife, so you could give the information to your best friend."

Edgar laughed at Layla's comment to his wife. Lynn frowned at him.

"I heard enough." She got up. "I had no idea you married a rude, conceited woman, Arius."

Layla got up too and Arius followed. "Better rude than a hypocrite." The two ladies took a step forward.

"Layla." Arius gave her the calming eyes. "Lynn, please sit down. You took the time to come and see me. We should catch up."

She eyed Layla and then sat down.

Arius kissed Layla on the cheek. "Could we please sit down, sweetheart?"

Layla sat back down. She saw the love Arius had for his sister and decided to make things right. "I am sorry, Lynn. The last thing I want to do is upset my husband. Family is important to him and we are a happy family."

Arius appreciated Layla being the bigger person to apologize. "Thank you, Layla. I appreciate that." He put his hand around her waist and gave her a hug.

Lynn has never seen her brother so affectionate before. "This is a new side to you, Arius. You have never been one to display public affection." Lynn said.

"Maybe, it took the right person to bring it out of me."

Layla was just loving Arius' replies. She put her head on his shoulder.

"How did you two meet?" Lynn started taking notes when Arius told her the same story, he told Layla's father. "It sounds like a spontaneous marriage."

"It sure was. We knew right away we were meant to be together," Layla added.

"I knew from our first encounter that Layla was the one."

"I was surprised when I heard you had a baby," the enquiring kept coming from Lynn.

"It happened right away. We got carried away from the first moment." Arius responded

"Moment or moments, honey?" They laughed.

Lynn did not get the joke.

"How are my nieces doing?" Arius asked Lynn.

"They are fine. Maya is three and Ellie almost two. I can't wait for you to see them at Kevin's Christmas Eve dinner party. Are you coming?"

"We need to discuss our plans first. Aunt Brianna are you cooking?" he asked.

"Layla and I could use a break. Plus, it has been a while since you saw everyone. It would be nice to go out."

Layla agreed with her. Arius was afraid because his ex-wife would be there.

"Edgar you have been quiet," Lynn said to her husband.

Edgar was too busy checking out Layla. "You know I am not much of a talker," Edgar said. "Arius, I am happy for you. You look like a new man. You deserve it."

Lynn faced tightened up. "Did you hear Sierra and Reginald have separated? Sierra left him." Lynn dropped the bomb on Layla.

"Sierra is not my business anymore. I have everything I need right here." He kissed Layla. The reaction Lynn was expecting from Arius, she did not get.

"We have got to go. I better see you next week." She hugged Arius.

Darius woke up from his nap calling dada. Arius picked him up.

"He is finally up. Let me see my nephew." Her eyes examined Darius's face.

"This is my son, Darius."

Layla could never get enough of Arius calling Darius his son.

"He must favor your family, Layla. He is a beautiful baby."

"Thank you, he does, but he is smart like his daddy."

"Wait, I see your jawline. That jawline runs in the family."

Arius found her comment amusing.

"Uncle Darius would have been happy you named your son after him."

"It was Layla's pick."

"It was nice meeting you, Layla." She put her hand out. Layla shook it. The ladies wanted to detest each other, but they both cared about Arius.

Aunt Brianna was quite entertained by Layla putting Lynn in her place. Even Arius was impressed by Layla's support of him.

"Layla, where have you been all our lives?" Aunt Brianna hugged Layla. "I can't wait for the dinner party."

"Auntie, there will be no trouble at the Christmas Eve dinner." Arius wanted no drama.

"Of course not. Auntie is just playing with you." Layla said in support of Aunt Brianna.

He gave them a firm look. "Thank you for taking up for me. You kept your word." Layla's face stiffened up. She was unable to hide her insecurities. Arius saw through her. "Auntie, could you please give us a few minutes." His aunt took Darius.

"Darius and I are going to watch the news." They left the room

"What's wrong?" Arius questioned Layla.

"Nothing is wrong."

He held her in his arms. "I know my wife. Talk to me."

"How do you feel about your ex being separated?"

"Layla, she is not my concern anymore. I am married to you."

"She was your first love. You told me if she left your cousin, then you would consider taking her back. What if she wants you back?"

"What Sierra wants is not important to me. You matter to me. Please don't ever doubt that." Arius attempted to reassure her.

"If you want to be with her, I will never get in your way. I care about you enough to let you go."

He was in disbelief. Where was the spunky woman he grew to adore? "Where is the determined woman who wouldn't quit to get my attention?"

"She is still here, but whenever I fought for someone that I cared about, I lost."

"Who? Your ex, Dexter?" Arius wondered when they would talk about him.

"I never spoke about him before because I did not want you to judge me based on my past mistakes."

"I would never judge you on your past mistakes because the woman you are today is all that matters."

Layla was tired of running away from her past. "When I left Brooklyn, I not only ran away from my obligations, but I also ran away from the woman I had become." She sat down. "I met Dexter at Gurdie's husband's birthday party. He was a friend of a friend. He was very smooth with his words. He could make you believe it was sunny outside when it was raining.

The only problem with him was," she hesitated for a moment. "He was married. I didn't usually date married men. Don't get me wrong, they pursued me and bought me expensive gifts, but I never got into a serious relationship with them. Anyway, he told me that his marriage was over with, but his wife refused to give him a divorce. He said that he was with her because of the kids, and he wanted to be with me."

"Did his wife find out about you?"

"More like I told her about us. I made his wife's life a living hell because he made me believe she stood in our way. I harassed her on the phone. I even keyed her car."

Arius was in disbelief. "Layla, this doesn't sound like you." She closed her eyes from humiliation. "This is not the woman I know."

"I buried that woman after I left home."

"How did the affair end?"

"I had no idea she was at the early stages of her pregnancy. She had a miscarriage from all the stress that I had caused her. Dexter finally came clean and told me that he loved his wife and family. I felt so bad about his wife losing the baby. I went through depression."

"That's why you agreed to marry Claude?"

She nodded. "And also, to become a surrogate to help a couple have a baby. I wanted to give a life back, after the life I had taken away."

"You are not completely at fault. Your ex deceived you into believing his wife was in the way of you being together."

"I should have made wiser decisions. I am prepared to make wiser decisions now. If you want to go back to your ex-wife, then I will set you free from our arrangement."

"I do not want to be set free. I am where I want to be." Arius knew she needed to hear much more than those words, but it was all he could say for now.

At that moment, he decided to reassure her in a more intimate way. He guided her to the bedroom. Arius undressed Layla and laid her on her stomach. He covered her shoulders with soft delicate kisses. Arius knew that was one of her sensitive spots. Layla moaned as her body quivered from agitation. Her body moved from side to side, not knowing how much more she could withstand. His hand covered her breasts so he could hold her in place. His fingers played her nipples like a guitar. Her hand reached to pet the beast. He was under her spell. Arius moved down the middle of her back where she lost all control.

"Oh my God, Arius. I don't know how much more I could take." That was Arius cue. He lifted up her leg as he entered her from behind. Layla felt like putty in his arms. He stroked her doubts away. She understood he was where he wanted to be.

CHAPTER 12

Ex vs Wife

The time has arrived for Arius to reveal his gift to Layla. He was beyond instigated when he saw the finished product. He fetched a clueless Layla who was preparing his lunch in the kitchen.

"Layla, Ricardo just informed me that the renovation is complete. I want to show it to you. I would like your honest opinion on their work."

"Let me finish making your favorite turkey, bacon, and avocado sandwich first."

Arius took the butterknife out of her hand. "Please, it will take a few minutes." He kissed her lips.

She has never seen Arius so excited before. "Alright."

His hand covered her eyes while she went downstairs.

"Is that necessary, Arius? I am going to break my neck." It was bad enough she was wearing her high heels, having no sight was an accident waiting to happen.

She got to the bottom step and Arius took a final look before removing his hand. "You can open your eyes now."

Nothing could prepare Layla for what she saw. It was more beautiful than any brand-named dress she has ever bought and definitely more priceless. She covered her mouth in admiration, as tears came out of her eyes.

"Welcome to Layla's Hair Salon." she read the bright pink neon sign. It was her own hair studio. Her lips wanted to move but they were taciturn.

Everything a salon needed was provided for her. There was a front desk to receive the clients, two styling chairs, two washing stations, and two hair dryers. Arius even enlarged a couple of her pictures with different hairdos from her phone.

"Arius, you did all this for me?" Layla murmured.

"My sweetheart always wanted to open her own hair salon. I hope I made your dream come true."

"You have." She ran into his arms. "You are the best husband ever."

"Does this prove that you are the only person I want to be with?"

"I am so sorry for ever doubting you."

"Great. Let me show you around. This is the waiting area with seats and a television. You have your own office. There is a bathroom and a small kitchen. Am I missing anything?" Arius scratched his head.

"It is perfect. You listened to everything I told you."

He relished in her happiness. "I have been listening to you since we started talking on the bus."

No man has ever gone out of their way to make Layla happy the way Arius has. Could it be possible he was in love with her? Just the thought of those words filled her with jubilation. She never believed any man would love her for the person she was inside, only outside.

"Thank you, thank you, thank you, honey." She covered his face with kisses of appreciation. Arius realized what a blessed man he was.

Layla got right to work to get the salon open by the first week of the new year. She placed orders for the necessary hair supplies and products that she would need before the opening in two weeks. She contacted Gurdie who was on board to help her out during the weekend. Arius was so impressed by Layla's business sense and her organization skills. He had faith in her future success.

With trying to juggle preparation for the grand opening, tending to Darius, and spending quality time with Arius; Layla was drained. Some nights, she laid back as Arius brought her to ecstasy. He was more interested with her needs being met than his own. Her happiness was a priority to him.

Layla appreciated everything Arius had done for her since he came into her life. He was a man of his word. Now it came time for her to hold her end of their arrangement at the Christmas Eve dinner party. It would be easy for her to do since she was his wife in every way. It wouldn't be a display of pretense, but a display of affection for the man she has grown to love.

The dinner party would either break or make their relationship. How would Arius react to seeing his first love? Would sparks fly again or would it finally close the chapter in their past. Layla tried hard to keep her insecurities under control.

On the day of the dinner party, a nervous Layla got dressed very carefully. She chose a Donna Karan red colored fitted wrap dress with ruffled sleeves up to her elbow. With her hair stylish skills, Layla colored her hair back to her natural light brown color and curled it out. Arius wore a Marc Jacobs black suit with a red tie to match Layla's outfit. They were a stunning couple.

By the time they got to the dinner party, everyone was already there. Arius made his grand entrance with his gorgeous wife by his side and his son in his arms. He went from the family fragile bird to the most envious man in the room. Layla was every man's fantasy, and she was all Arius. He introduced Layla to his family. Everyone could see how much he adored Layla and how much she was into him. Arius' brother approached the happy couple.

"Welcome back to New York, Arius. I am so happy to see you." His brother embraced him.

"Hi, Kevin. Long time no see." He turned to Layla to introduce her. "Kevin, this is my wife Layla."

Kevin and Layla looked awkward at each other.

"Do you two know each other?" Arius became nervous.

"Would you like to tell him?" Kevin suggested.

"We have a mutual friend. Kevin used to have a thing for Gurdie during our club-hopping days." Layla smiled.

"I wouldn't call it a thing. We used to be dancing friends." Kevin clarified.

"A dancing friend you wanted benefits from." Layla teased Kevin. "Seriously, it is good to see you again." Layla greeted him.

"How is Gurdie doing? It's been years since I saw her." Kevin inquired about his old crush.

"Your old dancing friend is now married with a little girl." She winked. "I can't believe you are Arius's brother. You two look nothing alike."

Kevin was a light-brown complexion with slanted light brown eyes. He had a jersey haircut and a goatee. Unlike Arius who was tall, he was averaged height.

"My little brother looks more like my mother's side of the family. I favor my handsome father's side."

"Very handsome." Layla kissed him.

Kevin started playing with Darius. "This is my little nephew. What a good-looking baby. He must resemble Layla's side of the family." He teased his brother. "Just kidding, I could see him looking more like you when he gets older. May I please hold him?" Darius went to his uncle and dropped his pacifier.

"He is so friendly. Hey, buddy."

Layla picked up the pacifier. "I better go and clean it. Where is the bathroom?" Layla asked.

"I could clean it." Arius insisted.

"Catch up with your brother. Where is the bathroom, Kevin?"

He instructed Layla to the bathroom. She found the bathroom, but it was occupied. Layla stood a few minutes in the hallway waiting for the person to come out. Finally, a slim, tall high yellow complexion lady came out of the bathroom with eyes on Layla.

The two ladies checked each other out hard. The lady approached Layla. She had an oval face with small eyes and a nose too large for her face. Her lips were pointy and pink. She tossed her blonde long cheap lace front wig to show Layla she had hair too. Little did she know, Layla's hair was real. She smirked at Layla.

"You must be the new Mrs. Colton." The lady said with her nose up in the air.

Layla put her hand on her hip. Let the fight begin. "You must be the adulterous ex." That's one for the wife.

"My name is Sierra to you. I see Arius got a young wife with a filthy mouth." One for the ex.

"My mouth isn't as filthy as your reputation."

Sierra's lips resembled a fish after that comment.

Layla studied the obnoxious woman. "Let's see, I must be a couple or more years younger than you. Don't hate me for my radiant appearance and youthful glow. You can thank Arius and his magic serum for that." Great come back by the wife. Layla could see the steam coming out of Sierra's ears.

"I had no idea Arius was into stuck up bitches who wear bootleg clothing." A weak point for the ex.

"That's your department with your scissor lips. He has upgraded to a beautiful, smart, stylish woman." Another blow by the wife. Layla looked down at Sierra's low budget JCPenney outfit.

"I know you heard a lot of things about me, but I am Arius's first love. When he is finished playing house with you, he will come back to me." Sierra attempts a comeback.

"Do you mean the house you were playing with his cousin?" Layla chuckled. "Now, that he has finished playing with you, you want to come back to a real man. That's not happening." Layla kept landing her punches.

"He will always be my husband. I made a mistake." A miserable miss by the ex.

"I kept asking myself why you would cheat on Arius. He is handsome, intelligent, charming and the skills he has in the bedroom are indescribable. No wonder you want him back." The hits were consistent from the wife.

"Everything you have is from the fruit of my labor." Sierra tries to salvage her dignity.

"You don't have enough balls to take all that credit." Layla just smacked her dignity away.

"You are only a sexual pleasure. I am his first love. You are nothing but a gold-digging bitch." Those three words always got the best of Layla. She has heard enough. She was ready to put Sierra in her place.

Lynn found the two ladies ready to rumble. "Sierra, what is going on here?" Lynn knew it was about to get offensive.

"Have you heard what this fresh bitch has been saying to me? Are you going to let her talk to me that way?" Sierra wanted back up.

"What are we back in high school? You need your friend to jump me." A nice upper blow landed by Layla.

"I am not going to jump anyone. I am a grown woman, and this is a family dinner," Lynn could see Layla had the advantage.

"I was telling Arius' temporary wife that she is for now and I am for the rest of Arius's life," Sierra explained.

"Sierra, that's outrageous. My brother will never go back to you after what you did to him." A new fighter has entered the ring.

"Whose side are you on? You have known me for years. Why are you taking for someone you don't even know?" Sierra wondered if she was getting double-teamed.

"I am on my brother's side. The way it should have always been." Lynn was not holding her tongue anymore.

"Family comes first," Layla added.

"Lynn, you saw the relationship I had with Arius. I was his everything. He used to walk on air when we were together. I am not a saint; I just made a mistake." Sierra did not know how long she could last while getting blows from both sides.

"A mistake is a kiss. You slept with Reginald, his best friend and then you left him. You did not care about him or your marriage."

Layla schooled Lynn right after their last conversation.

"Why are you making me look bad in front of her? She is a nobody." Sierra was ready to go down for the count.

"She is Arius' wife. I saw them together. He has life in him and a smile on his face again. Arius spoke to me without having tears in his eyes. I don't know her, but I know she has made my brother a happy man." Lynn truth landed Sierra on the ropes.

"Your brother loves me, and I used to make him happy." Sierra was completely in a daze by the blows Lynn was throwing.

"It was wrong what you did to Arius. I should have told you that a long time ago, instead of listening to your lame excuse of why you broke his heart."

Sierra searched for someone to throw in the towel. "Lynn, we have been friends since grade school. We are like sisters." At this point, Sierra felt like the underdog.

"I hooked you up with my brother. If you had respected our friendship, then you would have respected my brother and your marriage. Blood is thicker than water."

Sierra went down for the count. This was a humiliating knockout. She stumbled and stormed away.

"Thank you, Lynn." Layla underestimated Lynn's dissing abilities.

"You slapped me with some reality the other day. I should have spoken my mind a long time ago. I do love my brother and I want him to be happy."

Layla had a newfound respect for Lynn. "I promise you his happiness is my priority."

Could this be a truce between them, Lynn wondered? "Don't let me regret it. Enjoy your evening."

Layla had to pinch herself. Did her sister-in-law just give them her blessing? A new champion prevailed. The wife wins this battle by unanimous decision.

Arius searched the room with his eyes for Layla. He wondered what could be taking her so long to clean a pacifier. He was about to look for her when she returned. He saw the tension written on her face.

"Sweetheart, I was getting ready to come and find you," Arius stated.

"Let's just say your ex found me first and made a formal introduction."

"Was there any trouble?" he questioned.

"None that I couldn't handle. I see your ex is a very delusional woman."

"Should I worry about what just happened?"

"Are you worried about me or her?"

"Layla, what kind of question is that? I am worried you got into trouble."

"So, I am the one that gets into trouble. I went to clean Darius' pacifier, not start a fight with your ex." Was he taking for his ex, she thought?

"I didn't mean it that way." He put his arms around her. "I was worried about my wife. Trouble has a way of finding you. I will not tolerate anyone disrespecting you."

"I am sorry, honey. She just said some mean things to push my buttons and I gave as much as I got." Layla took a deep breath.

"I have no doubt about that, but you are here to spend time with my family. Not to defend our marriage to my ex. Let me go and talk to her." He could have imagined all the things Sierra told her.

"I fought my own battle and won. Let's forget about her and try to enjoy ourselves." Her only concern was her husband, not his desperate ex-wife.

"Have I told you how ravishing you look tonight."

"You did, but you can say it again, and again, and again."

He put his hand on the side of her butt.

"Honey, is that your hand I feel on my butt?" Layla got closer to him.

"Later, you are really going to feel more than my hand on your butt."

"And you are going to feel my hand on your-- "

Arius kissed her before she could say anymore. "Save your naughtiness for the after-party."

Kevin came into the room to announce it was time to eat. The festive food was depleted in an hour. After dinner, everyone had a story to share, but the most intriguing story was told by Arius. Layla never got tired of Arius telling the fantasy story of how they met. The only person not intrigued was Sierra. She got up and left the room. No one really missed her present.

The Kompa music started playing, and it did not take long for the dance floor to be filled with people. The beat had Layla shaking her shoulders. She wanted to dance with Arius, but Darius was sleeping in his arms.

"Arius, we should put Darius down to sleep in his car seat, so we can dance."

"He will not be comfortable in his car seat. He is already sleeping so peacefully in my arms."

Kevin overheard their discussion. "Arius, you could put him down in my room for a few minutes while you dance with your wife."

Layla batted her eyes at Arius. It didn't take much persuasion after that. He got up with Darius. "My wife always gets what she wants. I will be right back." He gave a cheery Layla a kiss.

Kevin showed him the way. Arius put Darius down and watched him sleep. He put pillows around him to protect him from falling and gushed over his precious sleeping face. As much as he was enjoying the moment, he sensed there was someone else in the room with him. He turned around to see a nervous Sierra staring at him.

"Hi, Arius," his ex-wife murmured.

"Sierra. What are you doing here?" Arius felt uncomfortable.

"I was hoping to have a few minutes with you alone."

His eyebrows went up from his uneasiness to be in the same room with a woman that brought him so much pain. "We have nothing to talk about." He tried to walk away.

She stood in front of him pleading, "Please, Arius. Give me a few minutes to hear what I have to say. Especially after your wife and Lynn told me off."

He saw the pathetic look on her face and decided to give her a few minutes of his time. "You have five minutes. My wife is waiting for me."

"Congratulations on your marriage. I watched you the whole night with your son. You are a good father. I am sorry we never got a chance to have any children." She seemed sincere, but he did not care for her kind words.

"Are you? You are such a hypocrite. You broke my heart after you slept with my cousin. He was my best friend. I remembered when I found you in bed with him. You weren't remorseful. You held your head high when you walked out the door."

"If I could take back that day, I would. You did not deserve such pain. I am so sorry."

"Now you are sorry. We went through a nasty divorce. Not one time you apologized to me. You didn't have any respect for me when you paraded around my family with your lover. You even pulled my sister in your dirty life."

"Our marriage wasn't perfect, and I felt you slipping away from me. You stopped making time for me."

"That gave you a reason to be with Reginald. I slipped away because you became distant with me. You moved away whenever I got close to you. I thought it was because you could not get pregnant." Sierra put her eyes down. "Now you show some sign of shame. Please tell me why you cheated on me."

"I have been living with my shame for the last few years. I wanted to reach out to you, so I could apologize. I never got enough courage." She struggled with her words. "It was selfish of me to take you for granted. Reginald made me laugh and told me how pretty I looked. He made me feel special when I needed to feel special. My stupid insecure reason made me lose my marriage."

"You are lying to me, Sierra. You have never been insecure. You have always been secure because your lighter complexion got you all the attention you needed. You could have cheated with any other man. Why my cousin and best friend?"

"You deserve the truth." She cleared her throat. "A week before Lynn set us up, I met Reginald at a party. He had a girlfriend, but we hit it off. We were very attracted to each other, but I refused to be any man's side chic. Lynn and I were like sisters. You and I have seen each other many times before and there was never any spark between us. Lynn wanted me to be her sister in every way. When she hooked us up, you were so nice and respectful towards me. In the past, I might have got the attention from men, but I never got respect. You gave it to me, and I fell for you."

"But it wasn't enough. You never got over, Reginald. How long was your affair?"

"After Reginald got dumped by his longtime girlfriend, we started to get to know each other better."

Arius was taken by this new revelation. "That was a couple of months after we got married."

She nodded. "He would stop by to see you when you were working in your office. Sometimes, he would be there an hour or two before I announced him."

"You had sex with him while I was working in my office?"

"No. We started to connect, and we would make out. We slept together when you were away for six weeks working on that project with Tyler Perry."

"Are you saying that you slept with my cousin four months after we got married?" Her deceitful eyes said it all. Arius was beyond stunned. The two people he trusted the most, lied to him from the very beginning. "You were with Reginald during our whole marriage?"

"I am so sorry, Arius."

"No reason for you to be sorry now. Thank you for finally telling me the truth. It is now time for both of us to move on with our new lives."

"Reginald left me because he said that I was still in love with you. When I heard you got married, I felt like someone put a dagger in my heart."

"I am blissful you know what it feels like."

"We have both experienced a broken heart, let's take the opportunity to help one another heal. Please give us a chance."

"You are the cause of my broken heart. Why would I give you another chance to rip my heart out of my chest, chew it up and spit it out again?"

"This time it will be different. We will value what we have."

"You are right about that. This time it is different because I am with someone who adores me. When she looks at me, I only see my reflection in her eyes. She laughs at my corny jokes. She asks me curious questions about my projects, and she pays attention to my answers. Whenever I enter a room, her face lights up and our son loves me so much. That is the new life I value."

"It hurts me to say, but I have never seen you so happy. I am glad you were given another chance at love. I just hope one day we can be friends."
"That will never happen."

Sierra lost every battle tonight. It finally took a toll on her. She started wailing.

Arius took a tissue out of Darius' bag to give to her. He put his arm around her shoulders to console her. She naturally went into his arms for comfort.

Layla opened the door to find Sierra and Arius in a sensual hold. She froze. Was her imagination playing tricks on her? So much came to her mind to explain the picture she was seeing. She knocked on the door to get their attention. Arius backed up. He noticed the tears that held her eyes hostage.

"You forgot Darius' pacifier." She swung the pacifier in the air. "It is getting late, I think we better take the baby home." Layla went around Arius and started dressing Darius.

"I was just coming out to dance with you," Arius said.

"It has been a long day. I want to go home." she said firmly.

"Excuse, me." Sierra left the room.

"Layla, please don't jump to the wrong conclusions. Nothing happened with me and Sierra."

"I want to go home." She picked up Darius and walked away.

"Whatever you want." Arius knew it was no use to persuade her to stay. Layla's wild imagination had jumped to the worst conclusion. A conclusion that may threaten their future.

CHAPTER 13

Say Those Words

The silent drive home even scared aunt Brianna. It was not like Layla to have nothing to say. Maybe coming face to face with Arius ex was not such a good idea after all. Arius feared this would push Layla over the edge.

If the drive home wasn't torture enough for Arius, seeing Layla go straight to her old room meant he was once again in the doghouse. Layla felt it was best for her to go to her old room to calm herself down while putting Darius to sleep. A once familiar room became an unfamiliar space after she moved into Arius's room. The wintry of the vacuous surrounding left her more dejected. The thought of Arius' arms around his ex-continued to torment her.

Arius paced back and forth searching for the right words to say to Layla. He wondered if he should give Layla some time alone or to march into the room to explain the misunderstanding that did not look so innocent. He thought about if he was in Layla's shoes, he would have probably reacted in the same way. Nevertheless, he was determined to make up with a flustered Layla. He opened the door to find a disquieted Layla staring out the window.

He approached her and attempted to put his arms around her. "Layla, there is no need for you to be in this room."

She moved away. "This is my room."

"This was your room. We sleep together now." He could see she had been crying.

"I just want some space and you can take the time to figure out what you want."

"Figure out what? If something is bothering you, then we need to talk about it. We decided a while back to live like a real married couple. We share the same room whether or not we are upset with each other."

"I do not want to share a room with someone who is clearly in love with someone else," the fearsome words finally came out of her mouth.

Arius was bewildered by her statement. "What are you talking about? I am not in love with Sierra. I am married to you."

"You did not say because you are in love with me. This is all about our arrangement. The arrangement we made for you to help me with my father and for me to help you get respect back from your family. We both held our end of the deal. Now we no longer need to be in a marriage anymore."

"Layla, you are talking nonsense. This is not the end of us or our marriage."

"You said that you are not in love with Sierra anymore, but you couldn't say you love me. I am not stupid."

"I haven't said it yet, but I have shown you how I feel for you. When the time is right, I will say those words to you." Those three words that he swore that he would never say again to protect his heart. Will he ever be ready to say it to Layla?

"When will that time be? When you realize that you are completely over Sierra? It only confirms that you do not feel it."

"No, you are wrong about that. I want to give you a heart that is completely healed. Not one that is broken."

Layla was stunned. "I thought Darius and I healed your heart by coming into your life. What has changed?"

"You and Darius have brought me so much happiness. I can't begin to describe. I just need some more time." The fear of saying those words overpowered Arius' feelings for Layla.

"More time?" This was a revelation Layla was not expecting. More time to be certain if he was with the right person? Layla was flabbergasted. "Take all the time you need while I sleep in my room."

"No! You are my wife, and I won't lose you because you think I am in love with a woman I would never give my heart to again. Sierra was crying and I gave her a tissue. Then she embraced me."

"You did not push her away. Her touch was familiar to you. You stayed in her embrace because you missed having her in your arms."

"Why would I miss a woman that took me down the darkest road I have ever been on? I am sorry I have not told you what you want to hear, but that doesn't mean I am still in love with Sierra."

"You cannot say something you do not feel."

"Do you know what I didn't feel last year at this time? I had nothing to be merry about. I ran away from my home and family." His thoughts flashed back to a sadness he never wanted to relive. "I was watching my uncle suffer in excruciating pain. I was sitting in a lifeless room staring at four empty walls. Never in a million years would I have imagined what I have now because I decided to play hero to a stranger. From the moment you took my seat, you stole my heart. I have not said the words you long to hear, but what I feel for you I have never felt for any woman. That is why I am so afraid of saying those words.

"Let me tell you what I have this year. I have a beautiful, sweet, sexy wife. I have the cutest son who adores me. I have respect and love from my family again. Do you know why?" Layla refused to give him eye contact. "It's all because of my sweetheart. Why would I want to be with anyone else?" She struggled with her emotions to keep from sobbing. "Sierra told me that she wanted me to give her another chance. She said that she would value our marriage this time. I told her that I value our marriage and the life that I have made with you and Darius."

"You value our marriage and our family?"

He took her into his arms. "I have valued every second since you came into my life."

"Sierra told me that I was for now and she was for the rest of your life."

"You are my life. I was dead before you came into my life." Arius kissed her gently.

In Layla's heart, she was certain Arius loved her, and she no longer needed to hear the words that she felt.

The anticipated day finally arrived. Layla ran around like a chicken without a head doing all the last-minute preparation for the opening. Gurdie got her hair braiding station ready. Aunt Brianna put out flyers and business cards for the clients to take with them after their visit. Layla looked around and everything was ready except for one thing. Where was Arius? She sprints upstairs looking for him.

"Arius, where are you?" Layla probed the house for him. It was almost time to open the door for the clients. She was about to run upstairs when Arius came into the house with her little sisters. The girls placed their overnight bags on the floor.

Layla ran to hug her sisters. "What are you girls doing here? Arius, I have been looking all over for you?"

"Arius said we could help you out and make fifty dollars a day." Lexie answered Layla."

"I thought you might need some extra hands. I spoke to your stepmother and she said it was okay."

Layla hugged him. "That was so thoughtful of you."

"Lexi will cover the front desk and Chana said she could shampoo hair and sweep hair off the floor. Of course, they will get paid."

"This will be our first real job." Lexie gave Chana a high five.

"Yes, it will," Layla smiled. "Thank you, honey for making all this possible. I have been looking all over for you. It is almost time to open the door."

"Great. I want to take a picture." Arius got his phone ready.

"I wanted you to be by my side. You made my dream come true."

He was so honored by her request. "I would love to be by your side."

She gave him a quick kiss before pulling him downstairs. The door was opened for the first few clients. Neither of them was expecting more than five people to come to the opening, but they had over eight ladies waiting.

Layla got right to work. She transformed Aunt Brianna's church friend from gospel ladies to glamourous ladies. Everyone was satisfied. Gurdie stunned her hair clients with flattery designs they never saw before. Chana got the hang of washing hair and Lexi made some friends at the front desk. She even got some tips from Aunt Brianna's church friends. Everyone contributed to a successful day.

By the end of the day, Layla was exhausted. She could barely keep her eyes open when she cleaned up. The room started to spin and then everything went black. The next thing Layla remembered was the feel of a damp towel on her head and hearing a voice telling her to wake up. She opened her eyes to a blur vision of Arius.

She shook her head to clear her vision. "What happened? What am I doing on the sectional?" Layla rubbed her temple.

"You fainted. You have a bump on the back of your head. You might have a concussion. What day is it? Who am I?"

"Arius! What kind of question is that?" She stumbled when she tried to get up.

He caught her in his arms. "Layla, please lay down and answer me."

She rested her head on the pillow. "Today is Saturday and you are my husband who has made me so very happy."

"Correction, I am your husband who loves you so much."

Besides seeing stars, she was now hearing things. "I do have a concussion."

"You heard me correctly, sweetheart. I love you."

"You don't have to tell me that you love me because I passed out."

"I said it because I meant it. I love you, Layla," he said convincingly.

She thought this was one of the many dreams she had about Arius telling her that he loves her.

"Layla, you are not hearing things. I love you."

She caressed him. "I thought I was dreaming. I waited for what seemed like forever for you to say those words to me." She gazed into his sincere eyes and saw all the love he had for her. "I love you so much."

"Why didn't you say it to me?"

"I didn't want to scare you away. I knew you weren't ready to hear it."

"I am sorry for taking so long to say it. Believe me when I tell you that I felt it from the moment I told you that you were going to be my wife."

"Even with all my naughtiness"

"Especially with all your naughtiness. How are you feeling, sweetheart?" Arius was so worried.

"I am fine. No need for you to worry about me. I haven't eaten all day."

"Why would you do something like that? You've been working for ten hours."

"I lost track of time."

"Please don't do that again. You were laying so helpless on the floor. I thought something was seriously wrong with you. I have lost too many people that I have loved to lose you too."

"Arius, you are not going to lose me. I am fine."

He took her into his arms and held her tight. Layla felt so emotional at that moment. The joyful tears came out.

"Why are you crying, my sweetheart?"

"I am so happy even with this very bad headache."

"You have a bump and a cut on the back of your head. You might need stitches."

"Don't be silly. All I need is some Tylenol and a band-aid. And most of all, your love."

He saw her cut was still bleeding. "You have my endless love, but your band-aid is soaked. You might have a concussion. I am not taking any chances. You are going to the hospital." Layla was too drained to argue with Arius.

The sterilized scent of the hospital room was not exactly the romantic setting Layla was expecting after Arius revealed his love to her. Maybe a room full of roses and lit strawberry candles. Regardless of the setting, she was with her husband who loved her.

The doctor examined Layla and she did not have a concussion. She did require a couple of stitches. He also ran a couple of tests and recommended that she stay overnight for observation. Arius was relieved when they admitted Layla. He wanted to make sure his sweetheart got the best of care.

The sun shined on Layla's face as she opened her eyes to see a sleepy Arius on the chair next to her. He was so worried about her that he decided to stay in the hospital with her. She checked the time and went into the bathroom. The door for the salon is supposed to open at noon. She took a shower and got dressed to leave. Arius was not going to let her leave without finding out her test results.

"I need to get home, Arius. We are supposed to open from twelve to four. I got stitches and the doctor said I do not have a concussion. What exactly am I wasting time here for?"

"Layla, we are going to wait for the test results. I need to know that you are fine."

"I don't need a doctor to tell me that if I work all day on an empty stomach, then I will pass out. It won't happen again."

"I will make sure of it. You are going to eat three meals every day."

"Thank you honey for worrying about me. It is so sweet of you, but it is not necessary." She hugged him.

The doctor entered the room with her test results. "I see my patient is ready to go." He looked at an eager Layla. "I have your test results with a couple of good news. I was worried you might be anemic, but you are not. Your iron level is good." They were cheerful with the first result. "The other good news is that you are pregnant." They both were silent.

"The test is incorrect, doctor. Tell him, Arius." Layla was perplexed.

"It is not possible. I cannot have children."

The doctor did not understand their reactions. "The blood test is accurate. I don't know what the situation is, but your wife is indeed pregnant."

"I have only slept with my husband." Layla was getting ready to put the doctor in his place.

"Layla, that is not what he meant." Arius tried to calm her.

"My husband was married before and his wife never got pregnant," Layla explained.

"That is correct, doctor," Arius confirmed.

"Did your doctor tell you what your problem was? Maybe it corrected itself." The doctor saw many cases like that.

"I never saw a doctor for my problem," Arius added.

"Your ex was probably on birth control pills the whole time you were married. Why do you think she got pregnant after she remarried?" Layla was beyond upset. Arius had nothing to say.

"I recommend that you make an appointment with your doctor as soon as possible. I am giving you a prescription for prenatal vitamins, please start taking it immediately. If you do not have a doctor, then the nurse will give you a few recommendations. Make sure to eat during the day or you will get lightheaded. Also get plenty of rest. Congratulations and good luck." They were too stunned to answer the doctor.

The tension was so thick driving back home, you could cut it with a knife. Layla wanted to scream profanity out of her mouth. She barely made it through her first pregnancy. Pregnancy and she did not mix. On the other hand, Arius wanted to scream for joy. He always dreamed of having children. Darius was his child in every way, but to have a child that shared his DNA would be priceless.

Aunt Brianna was happy to see them when they returned home. Layla said a quick hi and went to her room. She slammed the door. Arius decided not to go after her.

"Is Layla feeling better, Arius?" His aunt was concerned.

"Yes, she is. The doctor told her to get some rest and take her vitamins." Arius thought about all the names Layla was calling him now.

"Why is she upset? Is she anemic?"

"Not exactly," Arius questioned if he should inform his aunt about Layla's pregnancy. It wasn't exactly good news for Layla

"Arius, you are worrying me. What is wrong with Layla?" his aunt demanded.

"She is pregnant," he spits it out.

"As in going to have your baby. How is that possible?"

"It is possible Sierra was using birth control pills the whole time we were trying to have a baby. No wonder, she said that she was sorry we never had a chance to have children."

"Sierra was that deceitful." Aunt Brianna was in disbelief. "Regardless, that should be wonderful news for you."

"Layla told me she did not want to have any more children. I respected her decision. She had a horrible pregnancy experience with Darius. I think she hates me." Arius put his head down.

"She does not hate you. Layla is just in shock. This is great news."

"I am over the moon. I am going to have a baby with my wife, but she isn't exactly happy to be pregnant."

"She will come around. I am sure you will make this pregnancy experience a good one. Tell her all the ways you will make this pregnancy wonderful." She hugged Arius. "I am happy for both of you. I am going to make Layla's favorite pineapple upside-down cake to cheer her up. Now go upstairs and hug your pregnant wife."

"Maybe I should wait for the cake before going up."

His aunt pushed him out of the kitchen. On his way upstairs, Gurdie bumped into him.

"Is Layla in her room? Is she okay?" Gurdie queried.

"She is laying down. The doctor recommended that she gets plenty of rest and remember to eat during the day."

"Can I please see her?"

"Sure. Maybe you can cheer her up. I will get her something to eat." Arius went back downstairs.

Gurdie found Layla laying on her side. "Layla, are you sleeping?" she asked. Layla turned around. "Why do you look so gloomy? Did the doctor find something wrong with you?"

"Yes, he did. He said that I am pregnant." Layla's eyes filled with tears.

"I thought you told me that you were not having any more children."

"I thought Arius could not have kids. We have been having sex three to four times a day without using any protection. It turned out his ex was probably using contraceptives in order not to get pregnant. He believed he was infertile."

"Then it is good news for him."

"Not for me. Do you know what I went through when I was pregnant? I got all the symptoms, and I was unrecognizable."

"Layla, I am sure you were glowing. Your only problem was you did not have anyone to share the experience with you. This time you will have Arius. He loves and adores you."

"That doesn't matter. I will still be miserable."

"Layla, this isn't only about you. Your husband is probably happy that you are going to have his baby. You left your home to go to another state to have a stranger's baby. You are now pregnant for the man that loves you. The man you love. Be grateful for your blessing." Gurdie was always the word of wisdom.

"When did you mature and get so wise?"

"I have always been wise. Don't worry about working today. Your sisters and I have it covered. Take the week to rest and we can open up next weekend. We might have to open only for the weekends until you pass your first trimester. Your health comes first."

"Thanks, Gurdie. You are the best."

"That's what friends are for. I will tell Arius to get you a stool, so you don't stand on your feet all day. Get some rest." Gurdie gave her a big hug and went back to work.

An hour later, Arius came in with her lunch. Her favorite chicken salad sandwich, fruits, orange juice, and a big piece of cake. Layla felt bad about the way she reacted when the doctor told her she was pregnant. She saw the distressed in his eyes.

"How is my sweetheart doing? I brought you some lunch and auntie made your favorite cake." He placed the tray down on the nightstand. Guilt filled Layla.

"My head feels a little better." He sat next to her and kissed her head. "I am so sorry, honey."

"Everything is going to be alright. Do you want to talk, or do you want to listen to me say a few words?" She put her head on his shoulder to listen.

"I could imagine how surprised you are about our unexpected news, but I can't pretend that I am not elated. Darius will always be our first child, but my whole life I thought of having a house full of kids. I gave up on that dream when I couldn't get my ex pregnant. I truly believe that I was infertile. Then you came along and made my dream into reality. I respected the fact that you did not want to have more children. I know you had a horrible first pregnancy being alone with all the symptoms you had to live with. I promise you that you will have a better pregnancy with me.

"You will not spend one night crying yourself to sleep because I will find a way to put a smile on your face each and every day. I will run to the store in the middle of the night to get you whatever you are craving. I will massage your feet, back, and whatever aches you. I will buy you a special gift every month throughout your pregnancy to show you how much I appreciate you. I will tell you and show you constantly how beautiful you are to me. I will rub your belly with cocoa butter and vitamin E to reduce the appearance of stretch marks. We will schedule a c-section for you to preserve your valuable asset." Layla smiled. "If I missed anything, you could put it on the list."

By the time Arius was finished talking, Layla's face was covered with tears. Arius wiped her tears away. "Are those happy tears?"

"A lot of happy tears. I love you so much."

"I can't begin to tell you how much I love you."

"I love it when you show me." He got undressed and showed his pregnant wife just how much he loves and appreciates her.

CHAPTER 14

An Unexpected Revelation

Layla and Arius spent a couple of hours making love and celebrating their unplanned blessing. They desired to stay in bed the whole afternoon, but Arius had to take Lexie and Chana home. The warm soothing shower together was the perfect way to end their celebration. Nothing could ruin their splendid day. Until Layla opened the door for her father. She recalled his last visit and his indirect accusations. She was not thrilled to see him.

"Hi, Layla." Her father kissed her on the cheeks.

"Hi, Pop. What brings you here?"

"I came to pick up the girls."

"Arius was about to bring them home. You didn't have to come all this way." Layla was in no mood to be sociable.

"The girls told me that you had an accident. Is it so hard to believe that I was worried about you?" His eyes seemed sincere.

"Thank you for checking in on me and for letting Lexie and Chana come for the weekend. It was nice spending time with my sisters."

"You are a good big sister and definitely have matured for the better."

"Is that a compliment, Pop? Or am I delirious from the bump on my head?" Layla jeered.

"Very funny. I see your sarcastic husband is rubbing off on you."

"Then he must be doing something right," she smiled.

"You are in a permute mood for someone who was upset with me last time I saw you. Is everything alright?"

"Everything is fine. I passed out because I forgot to eat. The doctor said that I should eat and get plenty of rest." Layla felt it was best not to share her news with her father.

"Don't tell me your husband knocked you up again."

"Now I see where I get my filthy mouth from." Layla cackled.

"That's really funny." He sucked his teeth. "Hopefully, Arius will keep his hands off of you long enough for you to get some rest."

"I am more than a sexual partner to Arius. He loves me."

"You are right about that. It is written all over his blithe face." Her father took a seat. "Believe it or not, I am happy for you. I would like us to start with a clean slate. Can we give it a try?"

"How could we when you are always starting trouble for me? When are you going to stop looking down on me because my mother left you?"

"Your mother left us!" He raised his voice and then took a deep breath. "Let's not talk about your mother. I am proud of you and the woman you have become. The subject of your mother and me has been a touchy subject for us. I just want to forget your mother ever came into our lives."

"She still is my mother, and I will never forget her. Could you please tell me why my mother left us?"

"Could we put the past behind us? The last thing I want is for us to argue."

"Please, Pop. I need to know why she left us and why she never contacted me again?"

He didn't want to open a can of worms that would hurt more than heal, but he saw he had no choice. "If you insist, then I will tell you the truth. You are old enough to understand adult business. I am not perfect, Layla. Your mother had every reason to leave me." Her father was ready to confess to a secret he has been living with for far too long.

"You always made it seem like it was her fault. You told me that I was no good like her." Layla will never forget those painful words that cut deep in her soul.

"I am sorry. I was hurting. I felt like a loser."

"What does that mean?"

"Before your mother left me, I was having an affair with Fiona for almost three years."

An overwhelming feeling hit Layla instantly. "Three years? You mean before Chana was born."

He nodded. "When Fiona got pregnant, your mother told me to choose between her and my mistress. I deceived her for a couple of years about leaving Fiona. I wanted both of them in my life. When your mother found out I was still with Fiona, she was furious. Then she left me."

Layla felt the blood rushing to her head. "She left us because of your selfishness. You said that you met Fiona after mother left. Is Chana your daughter?" Could it be what she assumed for years was true?

"Yes, she is." Her father has seen that resentful look on Layla's face before.

"Unbelievable! You spent years saying horrible things about my mother and made her sound like a whore who left you for another man."

"I was embarrassed. All I could do is play the grieving husband and then I moved on with Fiona."

The truth hurt Layla more than the lie. "You are a filthy liar. If you were the cause of my mother leaving you, then why didn't she want anything to do with me?" The tears of anger overpowered Layla.

"Your mother wrote to me several times wanting you to join her in Florida. I never answered her letters. She even wrote to you and I never gave you the letters. Finally, I sent her a letter with a family picture we took at Lexie's baptism. You looked so happy with Lexie in your arms. She must've thought that you were better off without her.

Layla shook her head in disbelief. "How could you be so selfish? You kept me from being with my mother. Do you know how much pain I went through? I couldn't focus on school and then I partied my sorrows away. How could you be so evil?" Layla stood up to argue with him.

Arius came into the room after hearing Layla raise her voice. "Layla, why are you yelling? You shouldn't be upsetting yourself." He held her in his arms. "What have you said to my wife?"

"My daughter and I are having a discussion. You need to stay out of our business." Her father had enough of Arius interference.

"Layla is my wife and my business. What do you want me to do, Layla?" Arius was ready to deal with this problem once and for all.

"I want him to leave and I don't ever want to see him again," she demanded.

"I am going to get Lexie and Chana for you. Do not upset my wife again. She needs to rest and avoid stress like you."

Layla sat back down while Arius got the girls.

"Layla, you do not mean that. I am your father. Please forgive me," her father attempted to beg for her forgiveness.

"I will never forgive you. I am no longer your daughter. You are poison to me, and I won't let you ruin the good life I have here with Arius and Darius."

"What good life? Everything you have with your husband is a lie."

"How dare you call what I have with my husband a lie?"

"No one does a good deed for free. You hate me for arranging your marriage to Claude, but you accepted your husband buying you."

"What are you trying to say?"

"Your husband paid me more than generous for you."

"He paid you installments each month."

"He gave me fifty thousand dollars. Double what you owed me. When I stopped by to see you, he gave me more money to quiet me up. He has his own hidden agenda."

Layla had no idea Arius gave her father that much money. Arius entered the room with Lexie and Chana.

"What have I missed?" He has never seen such a cold expression on Layla's face.

"My father was just leaving. Thank you for helping me, Lexie and Chana."

"We want to help you every weekend. We made a hundred dollars each, plus tips. Could we please come back next weekend, daddy?" the girls asked their father. He had no answer for them.

"You are welcome whenever you want to come back," Layla answered for him. They gave Layla a big hug and then left.

Arius sat next to Layla. "Sweetheart, you should be resting, not arguing with your father." He kissed her forehead.

"I asked him about my mother and why she abandoned us."

"What did he say to you?"

"He told me she left him because he refused to leave his mistress Fiona who had a baby for him. He let me believe she left him for another man all these years."

"I am sorry, Layla. He had no right to lie to you."

She wondered what right her own husband had to lie to her. "What is your reason for lying to me?"

"What have I lied to you about?" Arius prayed it wasn't what he thought it was.

"You said that you paid my father with installments to clear my debt. Why did you give my father double the money I owed him? Did you buy me?"

"That's ridiculous! I paid your father double so he would never bother you for money again."

"Why didn't you tell me? And why did you pay him more money after that?"

"Your father tried to milk me for more money after you mentioned to him that I was paying him installments."

"You told me that before we got married. I believed you."

"I thought you would be mad at me for giving him all that money." Arius could not disguise the guilt on his face.

"Why would you do that for me? You didn't even know me." Layla felt there was more to Arius deception. "What are you keeping from me, Arius?"

Where should he begin? His deception was more overwhelming than she could ever imagine. "I made a promise to my uncle to help you. I had no idea how or if I would ever find you. I searched all over for you. I finally decided to go back home and then you indirectly found me."

"Did you promise your uncle that you would marry me?"

Arius put his head down in disgrace. "My uncle told me; he met the sweetest girl with a lot of spunk to her. The more he spoke about you, the more I found myself fascinated by you. In his will, he stated for me to find you and help you by any means. He believed that we could help each other."

"You turned your life around because your uncle told you to find and help me. This doesn't make any sense."

"My uncle called you Cindelala. He said you were a princess running from her evil father. He told me the first time he met you, you came into his room with a red dress and your hair smelled like a field of lilies. Your visits became the highlight of his day. He said that you reminded him of his first true love, Lalita. When you told him your story, it touched his heart. He never told me what you told him, except you ran away from New York to escape a miserable life. He felt there was an instant connection between you and me. I had a broken heart from my ex, and you had a broken heart from your father. The only thing that he omitted was you were pregnant.

"Before he got too sick to talk, he told me, if I wanted him to die a happy man, I must promise him that I would find you and follow his conditions in his will. My uncle has always kept all his promise to me, the least I could do is find Cindelala and help her. I went back to the nursing home to get information about you, but it was against the rules to release it. The only thing I had to go by was my uncle's information. He stated that you mentioned to him that you might leave Georgia in September to go back home. He said you came to Georgia on a Greyhound bus and you would probably leave the same way. He also said if you went back home, then you would be making the biggest mistake of your life.

"From the end of August to September, I spent going to the bus station in hopes of seeing you with no luck. I probably would have never found you because you had a baby. Finally, I decided to go back home, I was stunned when you told me who you were. I found Cindelala without even knowing it and she was sitting next to me on the bus."

"If you knew who I was, why didn't you tell me your intentions from the very beginning?"

"I tried to on the bus when I suggested we pretend to be a couple to help each other. It wasn't until I met your father, I came up with the arrangement."

"That still doesn't explain why you gave my father all that money and why you married me."

"Layla, I am not filthy rich, but I am comfortable when it comes to money. If you owed your father a hundred thousand dollars, I would have paid it. My uncle worked in the movie industry and he was wealthy. He wanted to help you through me. He only had the best intentions for us."

"How was he going to help us? Did you marry me to get money from your uncle?"

"I do not need my uncle's money. I have my own money. What my uncle wanted me to do, I had no intention of doing until I saw you had a baby. I changed my mind after that."

"What did you change your mind about?"

"In my uncle's will, he indicated for me to find you and marry you. My uncle believed you would be miserable if you did what your father expected of you, but he felt that we would be able to make each other happy."

"That's ridiculous. Why didn't you tell me?"

Arius would not answer her question.

"What are you not telling me, Arius?"

"The second part of my uncle's request is for us to stay married for two years in hope for us to fall in love." Arius was afraid to continue.

"What else?"

"After the two years, if we wanted to part ways, then you would get two million dollars."

"Why would you not tell me that part?" Arius remained quiet. "You didn't tell me because you thought I was a gold digger. You questioned me about my expensive wardrobe after we got married," Layla implied.

"It was a stupid innocent comment. I meant nothing by it, Layla. We are in a good place now. We are in love and expecting a baby. We are a happy family. Let's focus on the present and our bright future.

"You are not going to brush this under the rug. You declared your love to me. Why didn't you feel the need to tell me then or do you still believe I will leave you in two years because of the money?"

"I neglected to mention it to you because of my insecurities. I was afraid of getting hurt again. Yes, a part of me wanted you to be in the marriage because you loved me, not because of money."

"You think I am all about money because I have expensive clothes. What makes you think I would've married you at all? You had no right to make decisions for me like my father. You are no better than him."

"How could you compare me to your father? What I did was to benefit you and Darius."

"It benefits you too. You got a wife and now I am carrying your child."

"I got a wife because I took the time to get to know and love. You are carrying my child because it is a blessing, we both did not expect. Layla, could we please move forward?"

"No, you didn't trust me in the first place to tell me. Now, I am supposed to consider your feelings. You judged me based on my exterior. Maybe that is why you wanted to know about my inner soul."

"That is not the reason. I honestly wanted to get to know you because I liked you. Yes, I was protecting my broken heart. I was afraid of getting hurt again. I am sorry for keeping this from you. I love you Layla and you know I do."

"I don't know what to believe. I need some time to myself. I need to think about Darius and my future."

"I thought we had a future together. I thought we were a family. Do you want to leave me? Layla, please don't leave me."

"I am not leaving, but I want my space. I respected your wishes when you wanted to take things slowly. I need you to respect my wishes."

"You want to sleep in your room to punish me."

"I want to think without having any distractions from you."

"Is laying in my arms a distraction? Is kissing your neck a distraction? Is telling you I love you a distraction? Which one is the distraction?"

"Loving you is the distraction. I need to check on Darius." Layla went upstairs and Arius followed her.

"Do you want me to put Darius' crib in your room?"

"That won't be necessary." Layla found Darius sitting up in his crib. "What are you doing up, Boohbah?"

Darius rubbed his tired eyes fighting sleep. Layla took him out of the crib and started rocking him back to sleep.

"You can sleep in here with him. I could sleep in the guest room," Arius suggested.

"I will not change his environment because you can't tell me the truth. He is used to waking up and waiting for you to pick him up to put him between us."

"I love seeing his happy face in the morning. And yours too."

Layla loved seeing Arius face too. "I used to love buying pretty expensive things because it made me feel special and important. The feeling I did not have from any of my parents. Now the only pretty thing I love is his smile. Money is not important to me anymore."

"I am sorry for judging you. You are the most beautiful person I have ever met. inside and out."

"I am still mad at you, but I still love you. If I roll into your arms during the night, it is because my body is used to it."

"My arms will always welcome you."

"If I touch you during the night, don't make anything of it."

"Your touch is all I think about."

"Stop trying to soften me up."

"Is it alright for me to kiss you while you sleep, the way I always do?"

"Stop it, Arius. You are trying to make me lose focus."

"I could focus for both of us."

"Could you please put Darius back in his bed for me?" He gently placed Darius back in bed.

"Do you need anything before you go to sleep?"

"I want the husband that loves me to lay next to me and do all the things I like. The husband that kept the truth from me, I don't want to see him again."

Arius got in bed next to her. He kissed her lips as a sign of peace. "Only the husband that loves you is here to stay." Layla fell asleep peacefully in his arms knowing she could believe his words.

CHAPTER 15

Saved the Best Story for Last

Layla was so surprised how amazing her pregnancy was going. No symptoms except lightheadedness if she did not eat on time. She had no cravings and had less of an appetite than she had with her first pregnancy. She maintained all her natural beauty and the months went by fast thanks to Arius keeping all his promise to her.

Arius was the devoted father-to-be as he catered to all of Layla's needs. He massaged her aching back and feet every night since she worked six hours four days a week. The first time the baby kicked, Arius was applying cocoa butter on her belly when it happened. Layla has never seen a man glow as much as Arius did. The more he fell in love with the baby, the more Layla fell in love with him. To top it off, every month he got her one special present to celebrate a successful month.

In the middle of her eight-month, Arius had a very special surprise for Layla to put the biggest smile on her face during the July heatwave. He hoped this present would make her joyous beyond her belief. The present had arrived, and he could not wait to see her reaction.

Arius entered their bedroom to see Layla laying down in a red spaghetti strap dress with a tray of cheese and apples on her belly. Her vision melted his heart.

"What a beautiful picture!" Arius bent down and kissed Layla on her forehead. "I see you are enjoying your rest."

"Are you coming to join me? I would love the company." Layla moved down.

"I need you to please come downstairs with me."

"You told me to watch my show with my feet up. I am following your loving orders."

"I know what I said, but could you please come downstairs with me."

Layla looked at him as if he was crazy. "Arius, you told me to stop going up and down the stairs. The Real Housewives of Atlanta is really good. Nene and Kenya are about to set it off. I am not going downstairs."

"Your gift is here, and it is really big."

She struggled to jump out of bed with no success. "Nene and Kenya could wait. Please help me up, honey." She got some assistance from Arius. "Thank you, honey. Why didn't you mention my gift when you first came into the room, Arius? Is it a new car?"

"No, more priceless than a car. You are going to love it."

"I forgot, the car is the push gift," she said anxiously.

"You cannot get a push gift if you are having a c-section," Arius teased.

"What! A push gift is for delivering a baby. It does not matter how you do it," an agitated Layla replied.

"This is not the time to discuss your push gift. Let's go." Arius held her hand as she wobbled downstairs. When she got to the bottom of the stairs, she started sobbing.

Layla turned to Arius. "Arius, is this a dream?" She studied her gift.

"It is real and waiting for you."

"This is the most thoughtful gift you ever gave me." She saw someone she hasn't seen in over a decade.

"It's your mother. I didn't think you needed a red bow on this present."

The vision of her mother was still breathtaking. She was an older version of Layla with a flawless golden-brown complexion and a jet-black hair with some new growth gray hair. She had gained some weight since the last time Layla saw her, but she was still a glamorous woman. Her mother wore a coral-colored two-piece short sleeve linen suit and beige heels.

"Hi, Layla," her mother said in a soft voice.

"Mother, is it really you?" Layla attempted to pinch herself.

"Yes, it is."

Layla dashed into her mother's arms with her big belly. "It is so good to see your precious face again." They couldn't let go of their embrace.

Darius ran into the room screaming "mama".

"Who is this little man?" her mother asked.

"He is your grandson, Darius. Say hi to your grandma, Darius."

He examined her. "Hi," he said in a sweet voice.

"Give your grandma a hug." His little arms wrapped around his grandmother.

"That's a big hug. Look at all that hair. He has your father's eyes, and he is so beautiful. How old is he?" Her mother pats Darius' head.

"He just turned one in March and he started walking in May. He is our big boy," Layla said as she adored her son.

Darius jumped into Arius' arms. Aunt Brianna entered the room.

"Auntie, I want you to meet my mother. Mother, this is Arius' aunt Brianna." The two ladies greeted each other with a hug.

"Nice to meet you," Aunt Brianna stated in amazement. "The resemblance is striking between the two of you."

"Thank you. Everyone used to say I gave birth to my twin."

"Let's sit down," Arius suggested.

"I will get everyone something to drink." Aunt Brianna went to the kitchen. They sat down and Darius sat on Arius' lap.

"I am so rude. I forgot to introduce you to my husband, Arius."

"We are familiar with each other." He smiled at her mother.

"Arius got in touch with me a couple of weeks ago. He introduced himself as your husband and father of your children," her mother informed her.

"Honey, how did you find my mother?"

"I swallowed my pride and called your father for some information. He was very happy to give it to me, in hopes of making some brownie points with you. Then I hired a private detective."

"When Arius told me who he was, I almost had a heart attack. Finally, I was going to see my beautiful daughter and grandchild."

Layla stared at her mother. She looked the same, but you could see the years were catching up to her. "At first, I thought you abandoned me." Layla attempted to control her emotions by breathing in.

"I was so hurt by your father's deception that I ran. My heart was broken, and I thought the least your father would do is tell you the truth. I guess I was wrong," her mother said.

"He finally told me the truth in January. I haven't spoken to him since then."

"I would have taken you with me, but I left with enough money for a ticket to Florida. I lived with different relatives until I got settled. I contacted your father when I got a job. He never answered my calls and letters. Until I received a letter from your father telling me how happy you were and the picture of you holding your baby sister. I assumed that you hated me and was better off without me."

"Pop sent you that picture to hurt you. I do love my sisters, and they loved me for me. I felt unloved by both my parents. I needed you so much. Losing you took me down a dark path I never thought I would be able to turn back from." The dolefulness into Layla's eyes.

"Please don't be sad, Layla. That person brought you where you are today. We have so many good years ahead of us. Soon I will have two grandchildren. When are you due?" Her mother wanted to look forward, not back.

"Next month. We are so excited." Layla was elated to share their news.

"What are you having?" Her mother studied her growing belly.

"We are having a baby girl."

Arius kissed Layla. "We are very thrilled," he added.

"Then your family will be complete. Do you plan to have more kids?"

Arius backed away from that question.

Layla studied Arius's face. "We might have two more in a couple more years. Arius wants a house full of kids." That was the first time Layla ever mentioned having more kids.

Arius' smile said it all. Layla kissed him gently. Darius started fussing.

"You want a kiss too, Boohbah?" Layla kissed him and he hugged her face.

"I think he is hungry. I better get him his snack. Do you need anything, sweetheart?"

"Not yet. Thank you for asking. Eat all your snacks, Boohbah."

Her mother was amazed by the picture she was seeing. "I can't believe my daughter is married and a mommy. You look radiant, but you need to focus on yourself too," her mother recommended.

"I multitask. I am a wife, mother and business owner. I still workout, do my hair, and make myself pretty," Layla bragged.

"I could see that, but more kids. Two is enough."

"Mother, I didn't think I would have another baby after Darius. I had such a horrible pregnancy with him. It's different with this baby. Anything is possible with Arius by my side."

"I am sorry, Layla. It is not my place to give you advice."

"You are my mother. It will always be your place, but I will follow my heart."

"You are all grown up now. A wife and a mother. I am so proud of you."

"Thank you, mother. It means so much coming from you. There was a time I did not think it was possible for me to have a husband that loves me as much as Arius has or have a child look up at me the way Darius has. They both adore me."

"I am so happy for you. I thought about what I was going to say to you to make up for leaving you all these years. I wonder now, would your life have been the same if I did take you."

Layla considered what her mother said. She did not want to think of a life without Arius and Darius. "I would be miserable without Arius and Darius. They mean the world to me."

"I could see that."

"Did you remarry, mother?" Layla pondered about her mother's life while they were apart.

"I spent the first six years by myself. I couldn't trust men and I took the time to find myself. Your father treated me like a trophy wife to show to the world. He never took the time to get to know the real me. I guess that is why he got a mistress."

"Father got a mistress because he was selfish and greedy. He did not value what he had with you and our family. He allowed me to believe Chana was his stepdaughter all these years, while he bad mouthed you."

"Your father is old fashioned. He never expected me to leave him. He expected me to accept his mistress and his child. I knew I deserved better." She paused for a moment. "Five years ago, I met this wonderful guy. He is an average guy, and he respects me. His name is Felix. We have been married for three years."

"I am so happy for you, mother. I saw there was something different about you. Love agrees with you."

Aunt Brianna made a fresh pitcher of lemonade for Layla and her mother. She gave them each a glass.

"Thank you, auntie." Layla took a sip.

Arius came with her tray of cheese and apples.

"Here is your snack, sweetheart. I have some work to do in my office." He kissed her on the cheek.

"Thank you, honey. I love you."

"I love you too."

Layla watched him as he walked back to his office. "Auntie, why don't you sit down with us?" she asked.

"I am going to put Darius down for his nap in my room. I will come back in a few minutes to chat." Darius walked off with his auntie.

"You have such a lovely happy family, Layla," her mother complimented.
"We love each other. We can spend hours talking and laughing some nights.

"Aunt Brianna came back into the room. "I am back. Darius dozed off as soon as his head hit the pillow." she said.

"I was telling mother how much fun we have making each other laugh."

"Layla and Arius tell the craziest stories about their bus ride from Georgia."

"Auntie, why don't you tell my mother some of the stories. I need to tell Arius something. I will be back in a few minutes," Layla lifted herself off the couch.

"She'll be in there for a while," Aunt Brianna said. The ladies laugh.

Layla made her way to Arius' office.

He was not expecting her. "Layla, what are you doing here? You should be catching up with your mother." She embraced him. "What is that tender hug for?"

"You found my mother for me. You keep finding different ways to make me happy."

"The same way you make me happy every day. Remember when you woke up crying from the nightmare you had about never seeing your mother again." Layla nodded. "I watched you cry not knowing how to comfort you. I promised myself that I would never let you spend another night crying yourself to sleep. I felt like I let you down. That's when I decided to find your mother for you and put a smile back on your face again."

"You have put a very big smile on my face."

"The same smile you put on my face countless times."

"Like the smile I saw on your face when I said we will have a couple more kids."

"Are you sure about that?" Arius wanted to hear those confirming words.

"This pregnancy has been wonderful because of you. I am so happy and excited to see our baby. Now, I look forward to having many more children with you."

"Thank you, my sweetheart. You fill my heart with an enormous amount of love. I enjoyed sharing this pregnancy with you. What I wouldn't have done to share the first one with you."

"You are here now. That's all that matters. I have so much to thank you for."

"You could thank me later." He kissed her. "You should be spending time with your mother now."

"I don't even know how long she is staying."

"She is staying until the end of the week." Arius wished he had his camera to capture the expression on her face.

"Are you for real, Arius? My mother is going to spend the whole week with me." Layla gleamed in excitement.

"She is and at nighttime, you are all mine."

"What about now?" Her belly rubbed on him.

"Layla, we have company," Arius warned his frisky wife.

"My hormones make me so horny. Let's have a quickie." Layla started unzipping his pants.

"Layla!" Arius pants were already off.

"I am not wearing any underwear." She pushed him on the couch.

"How can I say no to that?"

Layla lifted up her dress and gave him a ride of appreciation.

Later that evening, Arius could not wait to have more quality time with Layla. He took a shower and hurried to their bedroom. Layla was so exhausted from her day with her mother. She laid half-naked on a long body pillow between her legs. Her long thick hair covered her breast and her full pink lips sent Arius a kiss when he came into the room.

"You are so sexy. I love your racy panties."

"Do not tease me about my granny panties. I need something to cover my big butt." Layla pulled her panties up her butt.

"I like it when your butt is uncovered."

"I am so hot even with the a/c on high. I can't even find a comfortable position." Layla struggled with the body pillow.

"Is your mother all settled in for the night?" Arius asked, but he was more focused on her naked body.

"She is fast asleep after her long day." Layla stopped struggling with the pillow when she felt the baby moving. "Come, Arius, your baby girl is working out again."

He jumped on the bed and saw her belly moving from side to side. He was amazed every time he saw his baby move. He placed his hand on her moving belly and she shifted from one side to the next. "Wow. She is stretching before her workout." He kissed her belly. "The miracle of life is so amazing."

"The baby is going to be up for a couple of hours kicking and moving."

"I will watch her while you sleep."

"How can I sleep with so much activity going on in my stomach, honey?"

He kissed her lips. "You only have three weeks left since you are having a c-section."

"Do you want me to have a natural birth?"

"It's your decision. I am worried about you getting cut up and the recovery time is longer."

Layla had the same concerns too. "I have been having nightmares about having a c-section. If something happens to me, then our children will have no mother and you no wife."

"Layla, nothing is going to happen to you. The doctors have done these procedures millions of times before. I am sure everything will be alright."

"You still didn't answer my question. Do you want me to have natural birth?"

"I would feel more comfortable with you having a natural birth. Your valuable asset was in good condition after Darius. I am sure it will be in perfect condition after our baby girl comes out. I heard you could do a vagina steaming to tighten up after birth. It all depends on how you care for yourself."

"You have been doing your research I see," she smiled.

"You and the baby's live matter to me. I don't want to lose either one of you. I just want you to have a safe delivery. The truth is your asset will always be valuable to me."

"I love you, honey." She kissed him.

"I love you too. I can't imagine my life without you. Could you please reconsider having a natural birth?"

"If it will make my husband happy, then I will think about it. The push gift better blow me away."

"I would love to talk about the push gift, but I am very distracted by your naked body." Arius pulled the pillow away from her legs. "I am the only body pillow you need."

"You are definitely more comfortable." She wrapped her legs around him.

"You know it is a scuffle to make love to you these days. I have no idea what I'm doing anymore."

"You are quite entertaining, honey." Layla giggles. She remembered him trying so hard not to crush her belly.

"It's not funny. I don't want to hurt you, but I want you so much."

"You could never hurt me. Let's do it from the back." She rolled over.

"That's easier for you to say." He removed her granny panties. His hand felt her wetness. "You are wet as usual, sweetheart."

"Wet and ready," she whispered. He accepted her invitation and entered her from the back. Every entry felt amazing to Arius. He stroked her so gently because he was afraid of hitting the baby's head. He kissed her all over her back as his hands covered her full breasts. Layla moaned in pure delight. She was already up to her second orgasm. Arius was not surprised when Layla started dozing off in the middle of their lovemaking. He always managed to make Layla snooze like a baby.

The weeks passed swiftly as Layla was a few days away from her due date. She struggled upstairs with her huge belly carrying her special package she has been waiting for. She needed a couple of things to complete her surprise. Her whole pregnancy, Arius gave her a present every month, now it was her turn to give him a special gift. When she finished preparing her gift, she struggled back down the stairs.

"Arius, it is here!" she shouted.

He sprints upstairs to get Layla's bag. He came back down out of breath. "Do you want me to get your pillow too?"

"Arius, I didn't say it is time. I said it is here," Layla chuckled.

"Layla, I feel like my heart is coming out of my mouth." He tried to catch his breath. "What is here?"

"Your special present." She revealed his present. It was Darius' framed birth certificate. Arius had signed the paternity papers for Darius. He was officially Darius' father. His new name was Darius Arius Colton.

"Wow!" He became tearful. "I have been his father since we met and seeing it on paper has made it so very real." He kissed Layla.

"I got two copies so you could put one up in your office."

"That's a great idea. Thank you, sweetheart." He hugged her.

"I wanted to get you something special for all those gifts you got me throughout my pregnancy."

"You and Darius coming into my life has been the greatest gift I ever got."

"I am going to hang it up in your office. By the way, auntie said that you have mail on the kitchen table." Arius picked up the envelope. It was a large yellow envelope from his uncle's lawyer. He opened it up and found a note on top of a sealed envelope.

The note said, '*Hi Arius, this is a letter from your uncle that he instructed me to give to you if you were to marry Cindelala. The letter got misplaced in your uncle's belongings at the nursing home. Sorry for the delay. I am sending it to you asap, Frank.*'

Arius sat down to read the letter.

My dearest son, Arius:

If you are reading this letter, then my life has expired. I hope this letter finds its way to you safely. Son, (I always considered you to be my son in every way.) I spent my whole life alone. All I had was my career to bring me joy. The only love I ever had was taken away from me. More and more, I saw you heading down the same lonely road I was on. You were hurt badly by your ex-wife's betrayal and you not being able to have children. It was very kind of you to come to take care of me and spend my last days with me. I know I will die loved and at peace

Before I go, I have one more story to share with you. I have told you about my love, Lalita, but I never told you the whole story. Lalita and I met when we were in college. We fell in love instantly, but her parents had arranged her marriage since she was a child. When we told them about our love, they forced her to break up with me. She was sad without me and found out she was pregnant with my child. We decided to be together and she left her family for me. On her way to be with me, she got into a fatal car accident. I felt like my heart died with her. I never loved again, but deep inside, I always wanted to have a child.

This story is going to sound like the most outrageous story I have ever told you, but it is very true. Just like you, I always wanted to have children, but after losing my true love; I lost hope of ever having love. One day, I did the craziest thing that would change my life forever. Two decades ago, I decided to freeze my semen so I could have a surrogate mother carry my child for me. As you can see, I never got the courage to go through with it. I continued to pay for it to be frozen every month. The months went by and then it turned to years. My lawyer informed me that the clinic got in contact with him about whether or not I wanted to continue to freeze it. I told him to tell them to discard it. My childbearing years are over.

A few weeks later, my lawyer informed me that there was a mistake in the clinic and my semen was used in a surrogate case. Apparently, the father and I had the same first initial and our last names were similar. They discarded his semen and mine was used to impregnate the surrogate mother. An honest mistake that saddened some people and benefited others. The young woman refused to abort and decided to carry the baby for adoption. The clinic would not release her name and she has no idea who I was. I remained anonymous and with the help of the clinic; I decided to cover her medical costs and find her baby a suitable parent. Of course, you came to mind. I knew you would be the perfect person to raise my child.

A month later, a young lady started working at the nursing home. The day this beautiful young lady came into my life, all the memories of Lalita came back to me. She resembled my late true love Lalita. She had those cat eyes that I was once in love with. I thought I was seeing a ghost. She was so radiant with such a bright spirit about her just like my Lalita. Her name is Layla, but I call her Cindelala. We became so close that I consider her the daughter I never had. She always took special care of me. I got to talking to her and she told me the craziest story. A story that was similar to mine. I was amazed to learn that her father had arranged a marriage for her. She also ran away from home a week before her wedding. It sounded so similar to Lalita's story.

A couple of weeks later, she told me she was carrying a child. The most amazing part is how she got pregnant. She told me about how she was going to be a surrogate for a couple, but the clinic got the semen's mix-up. I was shocked to learn that she was the young lady carrying my child. I never told her that I was the father. I spoke to her about her situation and I hoped that my words would help her make the right decision. When she started showing, it brought me so much joy that my baby was growing inside of her. She even let me feel the baby kick. That brought me so much happiness in my final months. Could it be this stranger who looked just like my Lalita was going to have my child? I often asked myself that question. What a coincidence!

I informed my lawyer, after she has the baby, if she decides to keep the baby, then I will give up my rights. If she decides to give up the baby for adoption, then I want you to adopt my son. Yes, I have a feeling it is a boy. I know you will be a good father. I have no idea what she will do, but if she decides to keep the baby, then I will include her in my will under the condition you find her. I want you to find her and get to know her the way I got to know her. She ran away from her evil father to gain his respect again. Help her and she will help you. Marry her and give it two years to see if you two can fall in love. If after two years, you two decide to part ways, then I will give her two million dollars. If you two decide to stay married, then I will leave my fortune to the happy couple and my heir will have his inheritance when he turns thirty under strict conditions.

I have already included what I have mentioned to you with my lawyer. He has instructions not to inform you about me being the father of Cindelala's baby or these conditions until you met my guidelines. Please keep your promise to me and marry Cindelala.

P.S. I saved the best story for last. I hope you enjoyed it. Let yourself love again and be loved. I will always watch over my beautiful family. I will love you always.

Uncle Darius

Arius put the letter down and tears rolled out of his eyes. Aunt Brianna came into the kitchen and tried to comfort him.

"What's wrong, Arius? Is it bad news?" He handed her the letter. She took a seat as she read the letter. She was astonished after reading it. "This cannot be true. Do you believe it?"

Before Arius could answer her, Layla came into the kitchen. Everyone looked gloomy.

"Arius, why are you crying? Did my gift touch you that much?" She put her arms around his shoulder. He debated whether to show her the letter. He decided to let her read it.

Layla read the letter. "Arius!" She dropped the letter on the floor. "It's time, Arius." The kitchen floor was wet. Her water broke.

Arius hurried to get her bag. "Auntie, please watch Darius for us."

"Layla, have a safe delivery." Aunt Brianna hugged Layla.

"Thank you, auntie. See you soon and hug Darius for me." Arius got Layla to the hospital faster than a speeding bullet.

Two hours later, Layla delivered her daughter through her valuable asset. She was as pink as could be with her mommy's face. They named her Aria Layla Colton. Arius could not contain his elation. He cried like a baby. His baby girl was finally here, and it was all possible because of his beautiful wife. He kissed Layla's precious lips and she never felt so loved.

CHAPTER 16

Happily, Ever After

The sweet scent of baby lotion traveled up Layla's nose, as she snuggled with her little princess in her arms while she breastfeeds her. She adored those special moments with her. The thought of her not having any more children after Darius completely disappeared with one look at Aria. Her precious face made her want to have many more babies. Arius would definitely be onboard with that idea. He hasn't stopped fussing over Aria since they got home from the hospital. She was his little princess.

Arius stood in the doorway with Layla's breakfast watching her feed the baby. He has seen this treasured image for the past two weeks and it never gets old. His beautiful wife feeding his little princess. He felt like the richest man in the world.

Layla sensed she was being watched. She put on her head and their eyes met. He sent her an air kiss and she caught it in her hand. "You are here right on time. Your little princess is finished eating. Time for daddy to burp her."

He put the tray down and put some hand sanitizer on his hands. He gushed at his baby sweet face while he picked her up. "I swear her face lights up whenever she sees me." Arius gazed into Aria's caramel brown eyes before putting her on his shoulder.

"Of course, it lights up. You are her daddy who spoils her with so much love." Layla commented.

"She is the most beautiful baby I have ever seen besides Darius. I love her so much." He rubbed her back gently, as Aria released a burp. "She just burped."

"It takes me a few minutes to burp her and she does it in a few seconds for you. That's daddy's little girl."

Arius sat down next to Layla on the bed. "She is so precious. Did we really make her?" Arius was stunned by their little creation.

"Yes, we did. I feel like making a hundred more because of her. It's like staring at my mini-me."

"Absolutely breathtaking." He kissed Layla. "You were amazing. Aria popped right out."

"Thank goodness she was only six pounds and nine ounces. Darius was almost nine pounds."

"That means your asset is still valuable." Arius jokes.

"Honey, are you wondering about my asset?" Layla batted her eyes at Arius. "My valuable asset is on vacation for the next four more weeks."

"Yet you keep grabbing on me."

Layla stroked his legs. "I miss my husband." Her seductive eyes toyed with him.

"I miss you too. The four weeks will go by so fast. I could see you being very creative until the time comes."

"Are you trying to put ideas in my head, honey?" She put her hand under his shirt.

"Layla, I could barely watch you breastfeed, so you could imagine what your touch is doing to me." His body trembled.

"I still have to thank you for my push gift."

Arius gave her a gold Mercedes-Benz. "Trust me, we are even. My gift cannot compare to my precious baby girl." Arius wanted so much to bring up his uncle's letter, but he did not want to upset Layla.

"What's on your mind, honey?" She put her hand in his hair.

"We haven't discussed my uncle's letter yet. I don't want to stress you out."

"We do need to discuss it and auntie is waiting for her quality time with Aria. Those four hours are so helpful for me to catch up on some sleep."

"Does she need to change her?"

"I just fed and changed her. In a couple of hours, she will be hungry again. There are a couple of bottles in the fridge."

"She is all set then. Auntie has everything she needs in her room. Say bye, bye to mommy, Aria." Layla gave her a kiss before they left.

Minutes later, Arius came back to the room. He doted on his lovely wife who was eating her breakfast. He often asked himself what he did to deserve such a happy, loving life. Arius allowed Layla to finish eating her breakfast before talking about his uncle's letter.

"Thank you, honey. This breakfast was so filling. If I had more energy, I would go and workout."

"You have plenty of time to work out. Plus, your stomach is already flat. You carried completely in your belly. Now all you need to do is tend to the baby and get plenty of rest. Anyway, auntie and I enjoy taking care of you."

"You are doing a great job." She kissed his cheek.

"If you don't want to talk about the letter, then we don't have to."

"I am sure the letter made my water break. As I read it, I felt my heart racing. I was completely stunned. I only knew your uncle's first name. The couple's name was Culton. Dennis and Valerie Culton. They were so devastated after they found out about the mix-up. They were holding on to that final hope that the baby might be theirs, so they ran a DNA test after I gave birth. My heart was beating so fast as we waited for the results. By that time, I was already in love with little Darius. When they got the result, they were very disappointed. I had to hold in my joy. I am not sure I would have allowed them to take him anyway."

"You fell in love with your baby. It would have been hard for you to give up your son."

"All the time that I spent with your uncle helped me develop feelings for a baby I was too afraid and immature to love. I started to appreciate his kicks and movements. When little Darius came, I saw my life in a new light. I thought about your uncle telling me that I was going to be a good mother, and everything was going to be alright. He believed in me when no one else did."

"My uncle died knowing that a woman who resembled his true love was going to have his baby."

"That's why I gave Darius a name that I truly felt was meant for him."

"The name he deserved."

"I am so sorry that Uncle Darius did not get a chance to see his baby. I waited for him to turn two months old because I was so worried about him catching a cold. When I went to the nursing home, your uncle's bed was empty. The attendee told me that he went to the hospital. I should have found out what hospital. I was so busy trying to be a good mother. I am sorry, Arius." Layla cried on his shoulder.

"Layla, please do not blame yourself. You were a new mother and alone in a city where you had no family. You were going through your own tribulations when my uncle was fighting for his life. My uncle brought us together that September morning. I was going through so much with my uncle's death and the life that I had to go back to. I usually mind my own business, but I took the time to help a woman I didn't even know. When you turned around and told me that you could fight your own battles, professor, I was so captivated by your beauty and guts. Then you took my seat and stole my heart away."

"Oh, honey." She kissed him. "I hated it when the bus got to Times Square. I was afraid that I wasn't going to see you again."

"I knew in my heart that you were going to be a part of my life. I just didn't know how until I rescued my princess from her evil father and made her my Queen."

"Thank you for rescuing me and becoming my superhero."

He kissed her. "Thank you for making me a happy man and father to our beautiful children."

"Last week, Lynn mentioned how much Darius is looking more like you."

"He is my son, of course he looks like me. Darius looks more like my father's side of the family every day. The Colton name lives on."

"Your uncle and Darius brought us together."

"My uncle will live on through him. He is a rich little boy."

"We are a family rich in love. Last year, the professor became my superhero. Today, you are my husband and the father of my children. Never in my wildest dreams would I have ever believed this would be my life."

"It is a blessing in disguise. I love you, my Cindelala."

"Not as much as I love you, my superhero." Arius embraced her in his loving arms. The bedroom light flashed on and off for a second. They both knew Uncle Darius was more than happy with their fairytale ending.

Thank you for reading 'The Arrangement', I hope you enjoyed this fun-loving book. I had a blast writing it.

Here is a sneak peek to my Summer Love Series, which starts with Book 1, An Unexpected Love. When two childhood friends find each other after years of being apart, they didn't expect the unexpected to bring them together. Jackson Marks, the handsome successful bachelor learned how to love someone more than himself. Drucilla Summer learned how to trust in love again. Can they face all the obstacles that are thrown at them to accept the unexpected love?

A very chilly night for the second week of April. Drucilla couldn't believe that she let her little sister convince her to go out. The cold wind went right through her dress. She should have worn something much warmer, she thought.

They arrived at the Rhythm of the Night Club. It was the hottest club in downtown Brooklyn. People stood in line for hours waiting to get in. Thank goodness the bouncer was memorized by Drucilla's revealing cleavage and let them in fast.

The club was packed on a Saturday night. It was oldies night. The DJ was playing 80s and 90s music. People were dancing and getting their grooves on. Tia immediately went on her way to look for her boyfriend. Drucilla made her way to the bar for something to drink.

"Excuse me!" she shouted to get the bartender's attention.

The bartender saw the stunning beauty in front of him and gave her all his attention. "What would you like to drink, beautiful?" he asked.

"Can I get a Sprite please," she said.

"Anything for you, beautiful." The bartender left to get her drink.

As she waited, she noticed a tall, very handsome guy in his late twenties with a mocha complexion looking at her on the other side of the bar. She dazed off and caught herself staring into his eyes. Those eyes looked so familiar. Their eyes locked in a moment and Drucilla quickly snapped out of it. He got up and she hoped he was not coming to talk to her. The last thing she needed was for any man to make a play for her tonight.

Thank goodness the bartender returned with her drink. "Here is your drink, beautiful." he put the glass in front of her.

Drucilla was so thirsty that she took a sip before paying. She spat some of it back in the glass. "This is not Sprite." she said angrily.

"Sorry, ma'am. We only have 7UP," he replied.

"Now I am ma'am. That is rude--" before she could finish her sentence.

The tall gentleman who was locking eyes with her earlier, interrupted her by saying, "Jimmy, why don't you ask the young lady what she wants instead of 7UP?" He turned to Drucilla and smiled.

"Sorry for any inconvenience. Would you like anything else to drink?" The bartender seemed afraid of the guy.

"Yes, can I please have a ginger ale with no ice. Thank you," she said politely, as she puts the money on the counter.

"On the house, Jimmy." the tall guy insisted. Jimmy returned her money back and gave Drucilla her drink.

The guy examined her angelic face as her long hair cascaded down her back. He was captivated by her. "You look so familiar. I just can't seem to place the face." His eyes focused hard on face.

"Wow, is that the best pick up line that you could come up with?" Drucilla smirked.

"Trust me, if I was trying to pick you up, I would have done it ten minutes ago when you were checking me out."

His cockiness did not impress her. "You are full of yourself. I was not checking you out. You were staring at me." She rolled her eyes.

"I can't blame you. I got my good looks from my mother and my charms from my father."

Drucilla shook her head. "You are so conceited."

"All I have been trying to say is that you look like someone I used to know. Without the fresh mouth like you, but I would never forget her sweet face."

Those words sounded so familiar to her. There was only one person she knew that ever called her sweet. She turned to get a closer look at him revealing her swollen belly. His head went back.

"You never saw a pregnant lady before?" She wished she could zipper her jacket, but that was not an option.

"Yes, I have. I just thought you were extremely curvy." He checked out her popping breasts.

"Does extremely curvy mean fat?" She could not believe the nerve of this guy.

"In my book, extremely curvy means extremely sexy."

Drucilla's blushed in astonishment.

"I told you if I wanted to pick you up that I would have done it a long time ago."

"I don't even know why I am even talking to you." Drucilla picked up her drink to get ready to go.

"I was only kidding. Seriously, you look like someone I went to Junior High with. That's all I have been trying to say."

Drucilla studied his face in the dim lighting. He was a suave looking man. He was wearing the hell out of a steel gray two-piece suit and his shirt was unbuttoned just enough to reveal his upper chest. His downward-slanting eyes caught her eyes examining him. Those eyes were more than familiar to Drucilla.

"You do look familiar," she remarked, as she continued to examine his face.

"Who's using a line now?" They both laughed. His laughter was music to her ears. Could he be her childhood best friend? It has been fourteen years since she saw him. She remembered his big afro and now his face looked so matured with a Caesar haircut and a light goatee that complimented his face. He definitely transformed from the tallest kid in school to a dashing handsome man.

"Could it be? Did you go to Whitman Junior High?" She waited eagerly for his answer.
"Yes, I did. Drucilla Summer."

Her face lit up. It was Jackson, her best friend that stopped kids from bullying her. She was so blissed to see him that she gave him a big hug.

"Jackson! I can't believe after all these years I have found you. Or have you found me?" Her wish came true. They hugged and laughed.

“I kept my promise to you.”

Drucilla pushed him. “It sure took you long enough. I have missed you, Jackson...

MD JEAN-PIERRE

Has entered the romance novel scene with her first book, which happens to be the fifth book she has written. This includes a love series that consists of 4 books, to be released in the near future. Her mind is a paradise of love with the desire to evolve into best-selling romance novels. Currently, she lives in Windsor, Ontario with her seven kids, but she grew up in Brooklyn, New York.